Andy's Origins

The Andromalius Chronicles Vol. 1

By Kim Schubert

Cover Art By: Cristal Designs

https://cristaldesignsartwork.myportfolio.com/

Dearest Reader,

I feel the need to offer a warning of sorts. This novel gets dark, and the continuation of the series is going to continue that trend.

If you've read my previous books, first thank you, second, it's darker and took a few betas off guard.

With that said, I truly hope you decide to join me in this series. I'm personally in love Andy's evolution.

Table of Contents

Chapter 1

My head throbbed in time to my heart, with an ache that rested not in the center of my forehead, like the ones resulting from my usual overconsumption of ale. This one seared into the very fibers of matter resting underneath my skull, abusing not simply muscles. Talons had dragged against and through the organ that controlled me, potentially removing a piece.

The effort to open my crusted eyes was a pitiful display of weakness, as it drove the torment of my head to levels only … only … someone … had achieved previously. Who? The memory was slippery; shadowed figures and colors swirled in my mind's eye, but no story arrived with them.

My sight did arrive, though, revealing blinding white lights above me. My stomach chose that moment to revolt, launching its contents onto the white speckled floor beneath the metal bed. I clung to the railing as I heaved, unable to recall what my last meal had been, or the drink that had potentially accompanied it.

Wiping my mouth on the back of my hand brought my attention to itchy fabric, grating against my skin. Surprise warred inside of me as my fingers explored the irritation at the inside of my elbow. A thin tube disappeared under the skin, and I followed it back to the clear bag hanging on a tower, also metal.

I pulled the tube out with a jerk, not trusting whatever substance was being delivered and hoping that with its removal, the pain between my ears would dissipate. Blood dripped against the metal rail before slipping down onto the white bed sheets.

My gaze snapped to the door as it opened. "You aren't supposed to be awake yet," the woman in a pink shirt and pants informed me in a whisper, her eyes round in terror, complete with the alluring smell of fear. A low growl formed inside me and forced its way out toward her.

"SHE'S AWAKE!" The woman jumped from whispering to a scream that would have made the banshees proud.

The shriek amplified the pain in my head to unbearable levels. I moved off the bed, finding my legs steady enough to hold my weight. I was going to remove her tongue, and possibly a lung, for causing me such anguish. The anger and irritation bubbling up through the confusion were familiar, and I found comfort in their presence.

A man appeared behind the pink banshee, what I took as his usual pallor flushed, dark locks sweat-stained and sticking to his forehead. He slowly stepped into the room, one hand holding a wooden rectangle with a metal device securing loose sheets of paper. I slapped it from his hand.

"Oh, okay An-Andy, let-let's calm down. No, no need to ca-cause a scene," he stammered, ending on a high-pitched chuckle with a pathetic attempt to smile. But it didn't reach his eyes. I inhaled deeply, drawing in the sickly sweet smell of their commingling fear.

"Who is Andy?" I asked, my voice rough and novel to my ears. "Where am I?!" I demanded, tossing strength behind it.

His posture straightened, fear replaced by … shock? Uncertainty? I couldn't place which, and it irritated me. I was better than that. Slowly, the sweaty man's hands lowered. I was tempted to slit both their throats. Where was something to accomplish that end?

As I hesitated, the sweaty man was gaining confidence, slowly walking toward a circular table with a strange seat that he pulled out, gesturing to it with his hand.

2

"You are Andy," he stated without the nervous stammering, as though repeating the name would suddenly make it ring true to me. Was it true? Was that my name?

"And you are in a hospital. Please, please sit, so we can talk." He gestured to the seat again, this time patting it.

My brow stayed furrowed, my gut not trusting any of this.

"Who are you?" I asked, refusing to sit.

"I'm Doctor Garcia, and I've been treating you for head trauma," he offered with a less strained smile, easing himself into the seat he had previously patted. The pink banshee inched toward the door.

I tilted my head at him. "Head trauma?" I repeated.

He nodded excitedly, clasping his hands together. "Yes, you were found on the side of the road. Your skull had sustained substantial damage."

"How?" I asked.

He shrugged. "We don't know. I was hoping you could tell me."

"I remember nothing, healer," I growled.

"Doctor, I am a doctor."

I narrowed my gaze at him. "That's what I said."

He nodded, "Of course," then patted his knees and rose. "Well, since you are up and about, there is a change of clothing in the bathroom, where you can also shower." He chuckled at something he found funny. "I'll leave you to it."

I scowled at the pink banshee as she retreated from the room that held me contained. The healer—doctor—eagerly exited with her.

I stayed in the same threatening stance, searching my mind for a trace of the beating that the healer claimed I had received. Nothing. I couldn't even say to certainty if my name was indeed this "Andy." I didn't know if I was safe here. Nothing felt real, and all of it, this hospital and whatever world it was part of, felt wrong.

The anger kept me calm, focused. It was the only thing that felt familiar.

...

The shower was refreshing, the warm water endless and pleasant, even if I found myself constantly checking the door, feeling exposed and uncertain. The clothing left much to be desired, as I tied the cloth pants as tightly as possible. Still, they refused to stay where I put them. Infuriating.

Heaving a sigh, I looked into the foggy mirror, seeing thick strands of honey blond plastered to the head I saw there. Startling green eyes looked back at me, and I averted my gaze instead to the straight nose and full pink lips. With a tentative hand, I touched my lips and the ridge of my nose, still refusing to meet my own emerald gaze, emanating from a face I didn't recognize at all.

...

Doctor Garcia knocked on the door and entered, followed by two additional men in matching uniforms and matching metal decorating their chests. I stayed seated on my bed in my overly large pants, watching the trio intently.

"Andy, these are police officers, law enforcement, here to ask you a few questions." The doctor waved a hand at the navy-blue men and turned to leave.

"How do you know my name is Andy?" I asked. "If I was found on the side of the road, as you claim, who knew my name?"

Doctor Garcia blinked at me repeatedly. "I—I don't know. One of the nurses reported it to me. I'll go find out," he exclaimed, making a hasty exit. I didn't believe him, and my narrowed gaze on his departing girth conveyed as much.

My gaze swung to the two in matching navy uniforms. They moved with a predator's grace I recognized.

"Who are you?" I asked, turning my probing gaze to each in turn.

4

"Police officers. I am Officer Davis, and this is Officer Brown." He made the introductions while watching me closely, pausing for a moment with his thumbs sticking into a thick belt with various items hanging from it. "We need to know everything you remember before your accident."

I tiled my head, "What accident?"

Officer Davis nodded, looking at Officer Brown. "Do you recall how you got to the highway?"

"How I got where?" I asked.

He nodded again. "How about where you work?"

"What is work?"

Now Officer Brown tried, "Do you have any family? A father? Brother? Who might be looking for you?"

That question made me ask a few of my own in my head. *Who would miss me? Would anyone?*

I turned my gaze to him, this time offering an actual answer. "I don't remember."

The navy-clad men shared a meaningful glance before nodding and leaving the room. What did that mean? And what was a highway?

...

I waited, having no idea what I was supposed to do and no one who cared to clarify such things. The pink banshee informed me that I needed to rest. I didn't feel particularly tired, although I did feel annoyed.

She touched a button on a black rectangle that hung from the wall. Pictures leapt to life, men and women speaking at me, various pictures of events happening. Everyone had small rectangular devices in their hands as well, laughing at them, talking into them. I had no reference for what sorcery this was, but the box hurt my head so I demanded that she end it or I would end her.

I sat in the uncomfortable, metal-framed bed and waited, knees pulled up to my chest, searching the depths of my mind for a glimmer of who I had been before. I was weak and exposed, and I enjoyed neither.

...

That was how the doctor found me, his gaze lingering on my hardly eaten food, which I had found lacking in ways I couldn't articulate, although texture was high on the list of issues.

"Doctor Garcia," I greeted him, inclining my head, noting his stiff posture and uneasy smile.

"Yes, Andy..." His facial expression faltered with renewed fear. I inhaled deeply, knowing the scent intimately. He began again with renewed vigor and a painfully stretched smile, "You are healing exceptionally well and ready to be discharged."

At my lack of response, he clarified, "You'll be able to leave now."

"How did you know my name?" I asked him again. There wouldn't be a third time.

"Liz—uh, Liz can answer that for you." He paled considerably as he gathered the lies he spewed. Such a pathetic creature for a healer. I found it all, and especially him, to be just so much confusion.

A woman walked into the room, and Doctor Garcia's expression blossomed fully into terror while he backed away from us both. She extended a hand to me. "Andy, I'm Liz. I'm your social worker."

I looked down at her hand and back to her, uncertain why she was holding it out. Yet her midnight gaze was familiar. I squinted at her and tilted my head, as though those actions alone would bring back the memories trapped somewhere inside of me.

Liz tucked a strand of brown hair behind her ear, adjusting her red spectacles. Her gaze faltered, but unlike the doctors, she looked worried, not fearful.

6

"How do you know what my name is?" I demanded.

Liz pursed her lips, coming to stand by the circular table, where she rested her satchel and paperwork. "I don't. I picked that name for you. It was better than Jane Doe," she chuckled.

"Who is Jane Doe?" I questioned.

The smile on Liz's painted red lips slipped. "No one," she sighed, shaking her head. "It doesn't matter, we don't know your real name and until you can tell us or we can find someone who knows you, Andy seemed an acceptable name."

"What is a social worker?" I questioned, accepting her answer on my borrowed name, for now. I didn't trust her, either.

Giving me a stiff smile, she motioned to the small table, sitting down and pulling paperwork from her satchel.

I slipped from the bed but refused to sit, arms crossed over my chest.

"I'm going to help arrange housing and a job for you, until your old memories return." She began pushing papers around in a meaningless heap.

"My memories will return?" I turned to her, actually feeling hopeful for a moment.

"Potentially. Possibly, hopefully," she answered with noncommittal shrug.

"When can we leave?" I demanded, ignoring the paperwork laid in front of me. Perhaps outside of this hospital, I'd find answers.

Liz smiled, holding out a writing instrument of some kind. "Once you sign the paperwork."

I had no idea how to sign a made-up name, and I was suspicious of all of it. But I was ready to do anything to escape from that room.

Chapter 2

"It's not much," Liz stated as we looked around the ... apartment unit, she had called it.

"Indeed, the level of cleanliness here is disturbing," I agreed.

Liz smiled, pulling out buckets of various items from beneath the sink. "Well, we can at least fix that."

She filled one bucket with warm water and a strong-smelling solution before handing it to me. "What do I do with this?" I questioned her.

She smirked. "Clean with it. Have you never cleaned before?"

I looked uncertainly into the soapy bubbles popping beneath my gaze, then back at her smug smile. "I don't know."

"Well, first time for everything," she responded, hoisting her own bucket of suds.

...

Several hours and one lesson in takeout ordering later, I was alone in the rundown apartment, which contained a couch, the black box called a TV, and a bed. I found it heavily lacking, although I was unable to define what was missing.

I sprawled on the uncomfortable bed, knowing something was exceptionally wrong with me, with worry eating my insides. Sleep was a long time coming.

...

"Money," Liz repeated the next morning, as we sat at a table in an eating establishment. Except it only served drinks, and not ale, but a brew called coffee.

"Gold?" I asked, narrowing my gaze at her.

She shook her head, pulling her purse from behind her on the chair. From a folded leather pouch, she pulled out green paper.

"Money," she repeated again, placing the paper on the table. "You'll need a job to earn money, so you can continue to drink coffee and buy food."

"Buy food? Not hunting?" I asked.

Liz laughed, a little too loud, "No, not hunting."

I nodded, blowing on the coffee that Liz assured me was delicious. Taking a hesitant sip, I grunted in surprise. "It's not terrible."

She laughed again, though her shrewd gaze had me wondering exactly what she was laughing at. "Wonderful. Now, what job skills do you have?"

I shrugged, "What are job skills?"

Liz nodded with a knowing smirk. What exactly was so entertaining for her? She adjusted her red glasses with the flared edges. "Do you know how to use a computer?"

"What's a computer?" I questioned.

Liz nodded, moving paperwork around in front of her. "I'm sure we can come up with something." The nodding seemed more to herself than to reassure me. I failed to see why I needed any of these skills.

"Perhaps an internship of sorts, to teach you the basics," she offered, rallying behind her idea with additional nodding.

"What's an internship?" I asked, taking another sip of the brew.

"Uh, well, you will shadow someone to learn skills in order to handle a job," Liz said, leaning into her own sip.

I watched her, my green meadow gaze never altering. "As you see fit," I finally decided on.

She cleared her throat before bubbling, "Great." Pushing papers from her large knapsack towards me, she explained, "This is where you need to be tomorrow. They'll help you get a wardrobe picked out and begin educating you on job skills." Liz smiled, but it didn't reach her eyes. Actually, her smiles never reached her muddy gaze, dark enough to appear black unless one sat and stared.

I nodded, looking down at the instructions, squinting as the black text solidified under my gaze. "Where is this street?" I asked.

Liz sighed, her mouth tightening as annoyance wafted from her. I inhaled deeply, scenting the emotion.

"A map, can you follow a map?" she clipped out.

"I can follow anything," I answered, refusing to break eye contact. Her muddy gaze widened, as she sat back quickly.

"Wonderful. I have another appointment. Let me know if you have any issues."

Her chair scraped loudly before she fled the coffee shop, her dull brown hair twitching in the wind. I was certain she wanted to check behind her for the danger that lurked there.

Danger that lurked there? Was I dangerous? I had been referring to myself. Why would I be a danger to her? A piercing behind my left eye had me dropping the brew to the table forgotten, then pressing against the pain. I hissed a breath out, knowing … knowing … WHAT? The pain intensified until I was left with unwanted tears streaming from the eye in question.

Slowly, the throbbing dulled to an ache, before retreating entirely.

Tossing the rest of the brew in the trash, I made my way back to the decrepit housing provided by Liz. I was unable to move past the wrongness of this whole situation.

…

The map proved to be the most useful item Liz had given me, not that she had given me much.

The exterior of the building was reminiscent of the ill-kept and rundown nature of my lodging. I sighed heavily, having expected something more elaborate. I squinted, tilting my head at the various shades of gray and brown, and finally at the red lettering announcing Job Center, peeling away in the sun.

Disappointment settled over me as I pushed through the aged glass door, a bell chiming merrily overhead. The interior was just as unsettling: a worn counter, piled with papers, in front of rows and rows of clothing.

A petite blonde emerged from said rows. "Good morning!" she greeted merrily. "You must be Andy. I'm Sara, it's so lovely to meet you."

Her warmth sounded genuine, prompting me to tilt my head, uncertainty flowing through me.

I looked down at her offered hand, then back to her blue gaze. She waited while I tested out the handshake Liz had attempted to teach me.

"Excellent grip," she smiled, her other hand covering our combined hands. I nodded at her, strange sensations unbuckling inside of me. Quickly, I dropped her hand.

"Let's get started," she proposed, looking me over with a critical eye. "I'm guessing you are a size six-ish, let's start there."

"What is a size six?" I asked, noting the strange softening in my voice. It felt wrong. I wasn't soft, ever. I couldn't say how I knew that, but I did.

"Oh, it's a clothing measurement. I'm a size two, but you've got height and hips on me," she tossed over her shoulder with a gentle smile.

I attempted a smile, the lifting of lips and creasing of eyes. It felt wrong and I was glad Sara didn't see it.

We stopped between two long racks of clothing, and Sara began quickly combing through the assorted items.

"You need everything, correct?" she asked, her attention not wavering from the variety of colors and cuts under her fingers.

"Define everything," I questioned, as I was doing constantly. I was still wearing the oversized pants and shirt from the hospital.

She paused, fingers delicately placed on the metal hanger. "Everything, as in all clothing items."

The silence stretched between us, my anger rising.

"It's okay," Sara said with a smile, melting the anger away. "Everything will include shorts, pants, tops, work attire, undergarments, and any accessories we have on hand." She snatched a red garment and held it up to me.

"I don't like red," I offered, brows furrowed. "I don't recall why," I added softly. The vulnerability clawing up my throat felt foreign.

Sara nodded, offering another understanding smile. The sensation of wrongness floated over me again, along with an odd sentiment I couldn't place.

...

After what felt like a monumental amount of time and borderline torture trying on the various garments, we had moved on to computers.

"I still fail to see the reasoning that this is more efficient than writing things down," I complained yet again, picking, as Sara had described it, at the keyboard.

"Well, when you get more experience at typing, this will be substantially faster." Her own patience, which had seemed expansive, was now gradually running out.

"Let's break for lunch?" she asked. "There's a killer sandwich shop around the corner, my treat!" she added perkily.

"Why is visiting a killer a treat?" I asked.

Sara stopped midstride after shouldering her small purse, barking out a shocked burst of laugher. "Let me try that again. Allow me to buy you lunch at a delicious sandwich shop."

"Oh, yes, that I understand," I nodded, following her out onto the crumbling sidewalk. "Although I admit, anything in this place that produced food would be suspect." I scanned the alleyway we passed, searching the shadows.

Sara shrugged, adjusting her purse on her shoulder. "There's always more than what first appears."

"Normally, more of the same," I disagreed.

She pulled open a worn wooden door. "After you," she motioned.

I nodded, walking in.

"We're going to need a conversation regarding manners," she muttered under her breath.

I craned a honey eyebrow at her comment.

"Sara!" an overweight man in a stained apron greeted her.

"Sergio!" she greeted gleefully back. "This is Andy. I was just raving to her about the delicious food here."

Sergio moved his wide girth surprisingly well through a narrow opening in the counter to hug Sara. He extended his hand and after only a brief hesitation, I took it.

"Welcome, welcome! Sergio always appreciates another beautiful young woman to dine on his excellent cuisine." He paused and I tilted my head, uncertain why he was still holding my hand. "Sorry, I fear I forget, uh...," he stammered.

"Andy," Sara said again, her laugh far too high-pitched to be comfortable.

I narrowed my eyes, releasing his overly extended handshake. "If you seek information, you should ask."

My comment was met with silence from the both of them.

"Andy is recovering from head trauma," Sara added cheerfully.

"Ah, I make something special for you, Andy! Sit! Sit!" the greasy man demanded.

I didn't enjoy being ordered around, but Sara eagerly pulled out two rusting chairs from under a yellowing table.

"I just telling Antonio he needs to settle down with a good girl like you," Sergio rambled on.

"Oh Sergio, Antonio has a lovely girlfriend!" Sara good-naturedly chided.

"Bah, spends all his money she does, on her damn phone all day, going to be influencer..."

I drummed my fingers on the table as the two bantered meaninglessly on.

...

"See? Told you, exquisite cuisine!" Sara beamed with a skip in her step. I suppose it was tolerable, although having had only three meals that I actually remembered, it didn't take much for one to make it into the top two. I stayed silent on that part.

But I did ask the other question on my mind. "Why does he give you free food?"

Sara cut a glance to me, and I saw for a moment the sharp stare she had mostly kept hidden behind warm smiles and easy laughs.

"We're friends," she stated simply.

"Hmmm. What do you do for him in turn?" I inquired. "Certainly, there is some sort of an exchange?"

14

Sara huffed out a laugh. "Like what, aside from my company and friendship?" she demanded sharply.

I shrugged. "I don't know. Thus far, I have only seen this world run on gold exchanges for goods. This is the first time I've seen a lack of coinage exchanged, but the goods still consumed."

"Sergio and I are friends," Sarah stated again, devoid of the joy she had previously carried in her tone. "He doesn't accept my money."

"Do you think he is trying to buy your goodwill, so you will mate with his son?" I asked seriously.

She stopped, mouth agape at me. "Andy, that's not how it is between us!"

I nodded, "My apologies, I simply didn't understand." I began walking again.

After a few steps and slow breaths, Sara tried again. "Maybe I'm not explaining myself correctly. We're friends. If Sergio needed something, I'd help him, no questions asked, because being friends implies a certain level of trust and…" she floundered.

"Exchanges that don't require monetary compensation?" I offered.

"Yes," she exclaimed, "exactly." She nodded, but I wasn't sure if it was to confirm the notion to me or to herself.

We finished the few blocks to the Job Center in silence. Unlocking the door, she gave me another winning smile. "Let's get back to tackling computer skills, before we call it a day."

"Of course," I agreed, with a bowed head and a feeling of empty resignation.

…

We were deep into the skill of copying and pasting when the bell overhanging the dirt-stained door announced another patron.

Sara checked her watch before mumbling, "Odd," pushing up to see who was there. I blinked dry eyes at the overly bright screen, stifling another complaint at the lunacy of this task.

I was tempted to eavesdrop on Sara; while she didn't give me the impression of someone who was hiding something, whatever she was doing had to be more interesting than the work I was currently tasked with.

To my surprise, I could hear her without really trying. I drummed my fingers against the worn plastic table, listening.

"I'm not going to say it again." Sara's voice had elevated, a hard edge attempting to override her fear. "You need to leave, Liam."

Liam's response was muffled, but I perked up, straightening in my chair.

"I'm serious, I have a whole room of people here. You need to leave," she repeated again. The tremble in her words was pathetic, although the fear coating my senses was delicious. I almost hated to interrupt, though I felt Liam and I might get along quite well.

Liam laughed. "Where is it, Sara? You don't take from us and not expect retribution. I've fucked you enough here to know that no one else is," he hissed. I found that sentiment to be accurate as well. Perhaps a job existed with this Liam that didn't involve computers.

"I don't know what you are talking about," Sara whimpered. "Get off, Liam. Please, you have to leave," she tried again.

I heard the thump of her body hitting something, "Don't try that fucking calming shit on me, you bitch! Where. Is. It?!" The thump recurred with each of his words.

On silent feet I stood, creeping out of the computer room and into the foyer with the worn desk and copious clothing. Liam had caged Sara against the loathsome counter, his smile dripping with cruelty from pristinely white teeth. Dark locks framed alluring eyes as his gaze caught my own emerald one.

16

I raised an eyebrow, taking in the others with him.

Each of the four goons surrounding Liam held a foul odor that didn't agree with my senses.

Liam's eyes narrowed, a surprising sign of intelligence as he raked his dark gaze over me.

"This is your entire room of people?" he mocked, his hands wrapped about Sara's biceps. He shook her, snapping her head back and forth.

Leaning close, he whispered into her ear. "We're going to have a good time with you two," he sneered, pulling back to press an unreturned kiss on her pale and drawn lips.

Something dark was bubbling up inside of me, a welcome coldness that spread from my middle and tingled as it spread down my legs and into my toes.

Liam nodded at one of his accomplices, who approached me with a wide gait as he took me in, eyes landing briefly on my own.

"You and me gunna have some fun, pretty." He twisted a hand into my hair. "Let's see what you can do with that mouth."

I laughed a full-body, gut-pleasing laugh, as anger twisted his features into something … else …

"You'll pay for that," he snarled.

Without a thought, my hand shot out and clamped around his throat, digits digging into the sensitive flesh as I pulled him closer. He gave up the hold on my hair. Foolish.

I drew him still closer, mimicking Liam's attempt at brutality. "Let me show you what this mouth can do," I hissed. Pinpricks of pain alighted in my gums before I snapped my mouth down onto this throat, the warm blood coating my mouth and stomach. Closing my teeth together, I snapped my head back, removing the front of his neck.

Frantically, he pressed against the open wound, leaking his life onto the soiled floor.

Blood oozing down my chin, I took in the hesitant forms of the other three.

My mouth opened and foreign words spilled out, ending in gleeful laughter as I pounced on the next fool. My body moved effortlessly, twisting perfectly to avoid a fist, kicking out precisely to render his idiotic form useless. Then, a twist of elegant hands, snapping a neck.

Liam had let go of Sara at this point, backing away, hands raised.

"What the fuck have you done, Sara?" he hissed.

"None of your fucking concern," she spat, shoving him out of the door. His remaining lackeys tried to follow but I was there, a clawed hand to the first one's heart, pulling out said appendage and letting his still-seeing eyes take in the wonder of my speed. The last one slipped by me while I was entranced with watching the other's soul leave the pathetic form of his body.

Dropping the now unbeating heart to the ground, I turned to Sara with a raised eyebrow. "Friends of yours?" I asked.

Her swallow was audible, her fear now directed towards me. "Let's get you washed up," she choked out.

I shrugged. The taint of blood had no ill effect upon me.

Chapter 3

I was washed with teeth brushed, dressed in one of the new outfits Sara had chosen for me earlier in the day. Apparently, this job center doubled as temporary housing. I exited the bathroom into a kitchen, far cleaner than the one I had been provided with, to find Liz and a man waiting for me.

"Who are you?" she demanded, the red-rimmed glasses gone, arms crossed over her chest, anger wafting from her.

I raised one caramel eyebrow at her, noting her tense posture as she stood inside the door.

"She asked you as question," the man next to her growled, leaning against the door frame, thick arms crossed across his chest. He smelled interesting, and I breathed deeply, trying to remember, willing myself to do so ... nothing. My frustration only grew.

"So she did," I answered, keeping his espresso gaze as I sat down at the kitchen table, lacing my fingers together on top of it. I had no fear of this guard she had dragged along behind her.

"I want an answer," Liz snapped out, stomping her pointed shoe on the ground to emphasize the point, chest heaving, lips pressed angrily together.

"Don't we all. At the moment, Liz, you know more about me than I do," I reminded her, not hiding how much that fucking irritated me.

The man standing next to Liz adjusted his stance, hands loose at his jeans-clad sides, no longer leaning.

"Why did you defend Sara?" Liz asked, attempting to soften her tone but failing.

I shrugged. "Did I defend Sara? Or did I take an easy opportunity to end life in a bloody and glorious way?" I tapped my chin, a small smile upon my lips.

"You need to get rid of her," the man snarled, turning to Liz.

"Where? Where the fuck do I put a demented killer?" she hissed back, not offering her eyes to the demented killer in question.

"There are things you aren't telling me," I confronted them.

"There are things you aren't telling us!" the man boomed. "Like what the fuck you are!"

"I am Andy. That is all I know," I snapped, my own voice rising. "And who gave you the authority to decide that, anyway?" I demanded of Liz.

"Just stay here. Zander, Sara, with me." Liz held up a hand, moving out of the room and taking the brown-eyed man and Sara with her. The door closed loudly before their footsteps faded.

I strained to hear them.

"You need to get rid of her," Zander demanded in hushed tones.

"We don't even know what she is," Liz pointed out.

"So how did you know her name?" Zander wasn't letting that point go.

"I didn't know it, I gave it to her."

"But why? Why Andy?"

Liz sighed, "You're going to laugh."

"Try me," Zander shot back.

"She reminded me of Andromalius."

Silence stretched out.

"Andromalius," Zander reverently whispered the name. "Why?"

"She accosted two different doctors before she fully regained consciousness, plus she's kind of a bitch. It felt fitting. Truthfully, I know nothing about her," Liz confessed on a sigh. "The hospital called me, since they thought she was one of us."

That explained the healer's reluctance to be in the same room as me, and the pink banshee's scream, but not who the "us" was.

"Sister, you tempt the Gods and all the monstrosities of Fae by naming her that," Zander admonished.

"Let them come, Zander. They don't know this world like we do," Liz snapped back.

Zander's long, drawn-out sigh was met with silence. Finally, he said, "Not this conversation again. We need to focus on this unknown Fae you've dragged into our midst."

"She sprouted claws and drank blood," Sara whispered in a hushed voice.

"That doesn't exactly narrow it down," Zander admitted.

"She did protect me," Sara offered.

"She would have killed you, had the mood struck her," Liz countered.

Sara cleared her throat. "Maybe, but she didn't, and she's an excellent fighter. I didn't even see her move, and hearts were being tossed out of bodies. We could use that."

"She's a danger, one we don't understand," Zander stated with conviction. "And she hasn't been forthcoming."

"It's possible that she truly doesn't remember," Sara offered. "Or, she just came from Fae."

Silence descended. Fae? Did that feel right? I was from Faery and I was Fae, I felt certain on that. But more, I was something more. The pain behind my right eye was only getting a grimace from me now. I wasn't giving in to the urge to press against it until it abated.

Show no weakness, whispered my soul.

"Let's take her to the pit," Zander decided. "It only allows others from Faery to enter."

"Who's going to fight her?" Sara demanded. "She just bit a Harker and killed it effortlessly. No one is going to touch her."

I couldn't help my smirk. Indeed, who would take on the unknown and untested Fae?

"I'll do it," Zander cockily supplied.

"The hell you will," hissed Liz.

"You're my sister, not my mother. Let's do this."

I stood waiting, anticipation running through my veins, the darkness inside of me spreading again, joyfully so.

The door opened. "You and me, we're going to fight."

"In the pit. Lead on," I grinned, standing to follow him.

He stalled, espresso eyes digging into me. "How did you know that?"

"You are loud. I heard you." I had decided on small words when communicating with the others.

Based on their surprise, it seemed not all Fae had my acute hearing.

...

The pit was adequately named. In the back of the ever-evolving Job Center was a massive dirt square, devoid of a floor and enclosed by stone walls. A few high, also grungy, windows let in natural light. Rings had been marked off with deep grooves in the dirt, while primitive wooden weapons lined one wall. I ran my fingers over the stone.

"This certainly is some place you have," I chuckled.

Zander made his way to the middle ring, tossing his shirt to Sara for safe keeping. Her fingers wrapped tightly around the white material, giving away her nerves.

Thick black lines encircled his arms, weaving a pattern around his thick biceps and up over his shoulders. His chest was well sculpted, with hard lines of well-earned muscle.

"See something you like?" he rumbled, cracking his neck, followed by his fingers.

I smiled, feeling the pin prick in my gums again. His eye landed on my mouth.

"That explains the Harker," he muttered.

I licked the tip of a fang protruding down. "Yes, it does," I growled deep in my throat.

Liz stood outside the circle, arms crossed, lips pressed tightly together.

I turned my attention back to Zander, about to ask when we should begin, when his bent body slammed into me. With arms around my waist, he took me to the ground with a thud.

I snapped my jaws close to his nose and he pulled back quickly, but I had already locked my legs around his waist, clenching my thighs.

"And here I thought you'd let me have the first hit," I hissed.

I released my ankles, only to slam my knee into his side, rolling and landing on top of him. I had a feeling Liz wouldn't take kindly to me breaking his nose, although why I should care eluded me. Plus, he was blocking that handsome face against my attack. I landed a punishing blow against his solar plexus.

Zander pumped his hips, catching me off guard and dislodging me. I landed, hands flat on either side of his head, breasts pushed into his face.

"Can't say I'm complaining about this," I laughed. His right hook to my side stated that he wasn't sharing my enjoyment.

With a grunt, I flipped up, waiting for him to stand before I attacked him in earnest. Jabs, kicks and haymakers landed and were deflected while we sized each other up in the dirt. He went low with a grab, and I kicked him soundly in the head.

Dazed, he looked up at me, before pouncing again. I will give credit to his stamina, for my own felt drained. I dodged left, attempting to land a blow to his stomach, only to have him catch my foot.

Something about this position felt familiar. I tilted my head, uncertainly flowing through me, before pain laced up my left eye. With a grunt, I ignored it.

No weakness. The smart move would be to snap my ankle; the fact that he didn't spoke volumes of his own vulnerability. I dropped my stance, ready to bring my other leg around, but he pulled me off balance, my calf now resting on his shoulder.

"Now, this is more my style," he growled, nipping dangerously close to my bottom lip.

With a snarl, I pushed away from him. The pounding behind my eye growing by the moment, I blinked through failing vision.

"Andy, what's wrong with your eyes?" Uncertainty glimmered in Zander's chocolate depths.

"I'm fine," I hissed, stumbling.

"You're fucking bleeding from both eyes!" he yelled, rather disgustedly. Such a waste of male talent, afraid of a little blood.

Show no weakness.

The pain split to both eyes and I dropped to my knees, panting. "I'm. Fine." I hissed out each word, willing my body to believe it.

Darkness took me, and it was an insult to my very core.

...

"Get up," a voice demanded.

Lying on my side, my own childlike whimpering meeting my ears, tears streaming down into the dirt below me, I doubted that I could do as ordered.

A booted foot connected with my midsection, taking away my breath, blurring my vision as blackness attempted to descend.

A hand snatched into the collar of my white training uniform, dragging me up. My gaze landed on my brother, sitting equally bloody and beaten on the side of the ring.

"Worthless," a voice muttered, as the hand tossed me to my knees. "Show no weakness, you pathetic whore."

He'd go for my brother next. I had to get up, I had to keep fighting him. The welcoming darkness wasn't an option.

I stood on trembling legs, facing the back of my abuser.

"I'm ready," I slurred out through a swollen and bleeding lip.

Chapter 4

I woke with the vision still hovering over me, not in a hospital room but in the pit. Gingerly, I touched my eyes, finding them healed from whatever had caused them ill.

Losing my sight was dangerous. I feared what it could mean for me.

"You're spelled," Zander announced as my gaze landed on him.

Gathering my thoughts took long moments, as I watched Zander leisurely leaning against the dirt-stained wall, his shirt returned to him.

"Define spelled?" I finally questioned, hesitantly. The whispered dream that had just played before my eyes felt real, giving me the sneaking suspicion that my memories were attempting to return. But I didn't trust him, didn't trust any of them.

Zander sighed, tossing his chestnut locks. "You've clearly pissed off someone with an exceptional grasp of magic, and that someone has spelled you to not remember, and potentially not access your own magic. But that part is impossible for us to know, since we didn't know what your power level was before the spelling."

"What are you?" I questioned, trying to get my legs under me.

"Fae," he offered.

"You don't trust me." It was a statement.

"I do not. Fae aren't known for being kind. They're known for amassing power, and destroying anything in their way." Zander's eyes unfocused with that statement.

"Who is Andromalius?"

His eyes snapped to me, refocusing with lightning speed. "No one."

"I find that hard to believe," I countered.

"No one I am ever going to discuss with you," he hissed. "Go home, someone will collect you tomorrow and find you a job."

I pulled myself up to my full height. "I don't enjoy being dismissed."

He held the door open for me. "Fae never do," he chuckled.

...

The entire situation ground on my nerves. Spelled to forget, being dismissed, not being able to have gold or green money to buy my own things. I had given up on the black box of the TV, instead turning my complete irritation toward the door as I waited for a summoning knock.

Pathetic.

The dream-memory plagued me. I had a brother. Was he alive? If so, was he trying to find me? Who was the man I fought as a child? Who was I? Where was Fae? Could I go back? Everything felt horridly askew, and nothing I did relieved the sensation. So I continued to wait.

...

Eons passed before the knock finally came. I pounced on the offending wooden structure, throwing it open, expecting Zander.

"Who are you?" I sagged, my anger leaving me in a rush.

"Why hello to you, too. I'm Bray, your guide to all things Fae in a human world." Bray's black hair was short, hints of blue streaked through it. "Are you going to offer me coffee?" she demanded, kicking the door open with her booted foot.

I shrugged, allowing her passage in her tattered jeans and black jacket. "I don't have any of the brew."

27

She rounded on me in shock. "You don't have coffee? How the fuck do you not have coffee?!"

"I don't have funds to procure it, and I have no idea how to make it," I admitted.

Bray opened and closed her mouth several times, before finally deciding how to proceed.

"Okay, you and me, Andy, are going to nab us a bad Fae, get you funds, and get you a fucking coffee pot. Clear?"

"What is 'nab'?"

"Catch, apprehend, bring to justice," Bray expanded.

"Justice?" I asked, following her from the ramshackle apartment I was forced to call home.

"Yeah, these Fae like to kill humans in new and fucked up ways." She shivered, tucking her hands into the jacket.

"And that's bad?" I clarified.

"Yeah, humans have no idea we are here—well, most of them, and that's the way it needs to stay. We can't have Fae going off the rails and killing whenever the fucking mood strikes." Her passion bled into her words.

"You protect humans?" I clarified. "And where is here?"

"Yes, I'm part human. And planet Earth," she answered, clearly beginning to question my mental faculties.

That caught my attention. "How?" I asked.

"Sweetie, I'm not here for a birds and bees conversation," Bray reprimanded.

"No, I mean how did the Fae not kill you?"

Bray rounded on me in the stairwell. "Why would the Fae kill me?"

"Half-breeds are forbidden."

I blinked. "How did I know that?" I wondered.

"Huh, how do you?" Bray asked, conspicuously not answering my original question.

"I don't know," I confessed, my brow furrowed. Confusion laid heavily on me. Bray shouldn't exist, and yet she did. Her status as a half-breed had me liking her far more than Liz, Sara, or Zander.

"Do you think half-breeds should be forbidden?" Bray asked, backing a step away.

It was my turn to not know how to proceed. "I don't think I care," I finally stated. "But I'm not certain."

"Kay, you suddenly get an urge to put a bullet between my eyes, please don't."

"What's a bullet?" I asked.

"Oh my fucking goodness, it's going to be a long day," Bray groaned.

....

Bray's office was in a slightly less decrepit part of town, although her vehicle required a great deal of improvement.

"Why do people drive these horseless things?" I asked as stepped out and shut the door, certain that the window might explode with the force needed. "And what does 'fucking' mean?"

She laughed heartily. "It's my favorite foul word, and also means getting busy, hiding the sausage..." she trailed off. "You get it. And as for the vehicle, efficiency. Not everyone can teleport, shift, or fly like the Fae," she dismissed me, while heading toward a towering building that spanned several of the city's blocks.

"Fae can fly?" I asked.

"So I'm told."

"You've never been?"

"Ha, no," she laughed bitterly, turning to me. "Half-breed, remember? Instant death sentence." With that, she resumed her long-legged stride toward the exceptionally clean glass doors ahead.

"Seth," she grunted at the doorman, who met my green gaze with his own cobalt one, and held it.

"Whatcha got here, Bray?" he asked, moving to block our way, towering a head over each of us, and just as powerfully wide.

"A newbie. Spelled, possibly powerful and my current partner," Bray shrugged, slipping her hands into her jacket pockets. "Why, what are you getting off of her?"

"Blood," Seth said, leaning closer and sniffing my throat.

"Kill anyone recently?" Bray asked, looking rather bored.

"Yes," I answered in a hiss.

"Oh shit, yeah, she dispatched two Harkers yesterday. Andy, have you not showered?" Bray asked with a disgusted look.

"Yes, I showered," I growled.

"What are you?" I asked, stepping closer to Seth, who quickly took a step back.

"He's a shifter," Bray answered. "Keep your parts put away." She grabbed my arm and ushered me through the door.

"What is a shifter?" I asked, head cranked around to watch Seth.

"Come back when I get off duty, and I'll show you." His smile conveyed lust, and I found myself smiling back.

"When does he get off?" I demanded of Bray.

"No," she stated as the elevator's doors closed.

30

"No what?" I questioned.

"You are not getting busy with Seth." She folded her arms over her chest. "No."

"Why not? He seems agreeable to the idea," I shrugged.

"Because he's a shifter, he's love 'em and leave 'em. Because I don't need that drama, and because I'm not getting in trouble with Liz because you accidentally killed him with your hunger."

The elevator doors slid smoothly open. "Hunger?" I questioned.

She unlocked a smooth wooden door carved with the golden words, "B. Services."

"Yes, if you are Fae, some feed by sex, and depending how long ago you last fed, you could easily drain him."

"Drain him?" I echoed, then laughed. "I think I made a joke, although I do fail to properly understand it."

Bray shook her head, moving to the small kitchen area and spooning ground coffee into a machine.

"You did. But I'm not explaining it. And again, no. Go practice your Fae hunger issues on someone else." She turned to me, arms crossed tensely over her jacket.

"Will I feel hungry?" I asked.

"I don't know."

"Do you?" I questioned.

"Not in the same way you would." Her answer left much to be discovered, but I found myself leaving it alone.

"What do we do now?" I was bored of the sitting. I far more enjoyed the killing.

"We wait for the coffee to finish."

"Why?"

"Because I need another damn cup to think properly," she grunted.

I sighed, "I don't understand the obsession with the brew."

"I know, here." She moved to the desks set up behind me. "Look over these files, tell me what you think."

...

The files were tightly worded, detailed descriptions of crimes committed against humans by a Fae, who was listed only as "assailant" or "murderer," never by a proper name or even the classification of Fae.

Bray was on her second cup when I finished.

"And?" I asked.

She choked on her sip. "And??" she parroted back.

"Fae kill humans. That's what they do," I shrugged. "Humans are weaker. I don't understand why the detailed rundown of how they were killed is necessary."

Bray's electric blue gaze met mine for a long time before she set down her beloved coffee, the only reason I knew this was going to be serious.

"Killing is bad," she began. I gave her a disbelieving stare. "Killing humans is bad," she attempted again.

"Why?" I demanded.

"Because they're innocent."

I scoffed, "An entire race is not innocent. While there may be innocents scattered among the many, death is deserved by most."

Bray blinked at me, attempting another line of attack. "Fae aren't supposed to be here. We need to keep a lid on them—us—being here. Going around

32

and killing everything human is bad, because it will alert humans to our presence."

"What do you think the humans are capable of doing to us if they knew we were here?" I asked.

"Testing, government labs, iron poisoning … bad stuff," Bray summed up.

"We could kill them all," I shrugged, seeing no issue with it, and not willing to waste time on what a government lab might entail.

"Kill an entire race? Eliminate them all…" The rest of her words were lost on me, as the pain behind my left eye flared up.

I made no attempt to hide it from her, pressing on the source.

"What's wrong?" she questioned, leaning forward for a better look at me.

"I don't know, my eyes hurt occasionally. Randomly," I admitted, even though it felt dangerous to admit a weakness to her.

She nodded. "It must be related to the spell, to keep you from getting too close to who you were."

I sighed, the pain easing as the conversation changed. "Why? Why spell me? Why not just kill me?"

"Maybe they couldn't kill you, maybe they needed you alive. Or maybe this is some fucked up form of torture for you?" She shrugged. "Look, I don't pretend to know why anything happens, but I can tell you, the only way to figure it out, is through."

"That's cryptic," I informed her, crossing my arms over my newly acquired graphic T, as Sara had called it.

She rolled her eyes. "Fae killing humans is bad. We get to hunt the bad ones."

"Define hunt," I asked hopefully, dropping my arms and leaning forward.

"Kill, maim, torture, or even feed from. We just need their heads to collect a bounty."

"Well now, that's lovely. Why didn't you just lead with that?"

Her blue-eyed stare was not amused.

...

"I dislike this waiting," I informed Bray for the three hundred and twentieth time.

"I know," she groaned.

"I wish to slay the offending Fae currently inside the brothel," I tried again.

"No."

"Okay, okay, it's a drinking establishment. I can drink there. I just can't kill there." Earlier, we'd had a long talk about what I was allowed to do and not do in bars. Fuck some stranger, yes; kill a Fae, no. Shower in the sink, also no.

"This is a frequent hangout of the Winter Court. We can't blow our cover," she hissed at me.

We had also had an in-depth conversation about the Courts of Fae, which followed the seasons.

I huffed out a breath. "I dislike this waiting."

Bray groaned. "We don't know his exact power level. According to everything that was reported, he's probably a five-ish out of ten. The ability to glamour himself is standard for all Fae, and the manners of killing didn't indicate any special powers." She sighed, "Just a penchant for ripping and stabbing."

"Do Liz and Zander do this waiting?" I questioned, not at all interested in the Fae power rating system.

Bray barked out a short laugh. "No, they're too powerful to bother with such a low-level job."

I grunted. "So they are a level 10? And what exactly are their jobs?" I was gathering that jobs were monumentally important on Earth. One had to obtain one in order to eat and purchase the brew so beloved by all.

Bray sighed, "Liz and Zander are in charge of helping Fae acclimate to Earth. They take care of any issues that may arise, and pay us to kill the bad Fae."

"Where do they obtain the gold for such an enterprise?" I questioned.

Bray didn't bother correcting my inaccurate use of "gold." Instead, she offered, "We pay them—I mean, the Fae pay them—to keep the peace, to keep us all safe here."

I grunted. "But Liz and Zander aren't the ones who actually enforce the rules or physically protect the Fae?" I was learning there was a big difference between being given information and things actually making sense.

...

Forty-seven minutes and an additional twelve dislikes of waiting later, the Fae emerged.

"He looks human," I muttered, wondering if Bray had made an error. Not that I was complaining. A kill was a kill.

"It's glamour," Bray hissed, exiting the car quietly. I followed her lead, although the creaking door surely had to give away our position.

"Remember—" she began in a hissed voice.

"I recall," I replied in a monotone. Her list of rules was excessive.

I stayed behind her. Apparently, being the one with the most knives and bullets gave her seniority or authority to go first. I still didn't understand why growing claws and fangs didn't count for just as much.

The brick alleyway that the Fae led us down was laced with human waste and foul-smelling trash. Bray pinched her nose closed, her usually robust complexion losing its warmth.

The alleyway continued to the next street, but we turned off to the right, following the Fae.

"When can we kill him?" I groaned. Certainly this was a torture, to continue the waiting while our prey was so close.

"Soon, and shut up!" she hissed back, leaning precariously close to the back side of a refuse container.

On a sigh, I looked up, noting the lack of a moon and stars. Looking back, I found only a solid brick wall. It took my brain a moment to catch up to what my eyes were seeing. We had just come from that direction, and now were trapped. Points to the Fae, I thought. Perhaps were weren't the hunters after all.

"Glamour," I whispered, turning to find Bray no longer at the refuse container.

The Fae, who hadn't seemed that impressive of a threat so far, now went up several levels in my own internal rating system.

Bray stood facing off against the human glamour of the Fae we had been hunting, saying something irrelevant, considering that the danger was behind her. From the glamoured shadows, a blackened, dry, and cracking tree limb descended to the ground. The entire tree-like shape then moved into my line of sight, red eyes securely fixed on its prey's back. It was front heavy, the long, arm-like appendages supporting its heavy girth, while short stumps for legs kept it from sliding along the glamoured, but still vile, stone ground. Such a clumsy form belonged in Fae and not on Earth, that much I knew.

"Hey, what the hell, Andy?!" Bray hissed, as I landed headed heavily on top of her, rolling us away. Her appalled berating was drowned out by the sound of the tree slamming into the stone of our previous position. Shards of rock sprayed us, biting into the flesh of our uncovered faces before we scrambled up.

"Oh, fuck." Her rounded blue gaze moved up the impossible heights of the tree beast. "Never mind, please continue," she amended, taking in the Fae in his true form.

36

"I thought you'd be taller, half-breed," he crooned at her, moving in a jerkily distorted manner, no longer slamming his tree arms into the stone, which made him annoyingly faster.

Instincts warned that one barbed appendage through the heart would be the end of me. Pathetic, was I really that easy to kill?

Only one way to find out.

The Fae hadn't paid much attention to me thus far, and based on his "half-breed" comment, I wasn't on tonight's menu. Fucking rude. Darting to the side, I headed behind the giant twig, pretending to run.

Ugh, that was a disgusting thought. Bray even called out a "What the hell?" before we began defending her life.

Ceasing my powerful momentum, I twisted, launching myself onto the twig-man's back, pulling back on the ramshackle leaves he wore on what I thought was a head.

"Hello, pretty," I whispered, using all my strength to yank backwards. I thought that strength considerable, but his head did not snap off as planned. Instead, with one swift flip, it sent me sprawling to the ground. Without even looking at my prone form, the Fae broke off an arm, pinning me to the ground with deadly accuracy through my stomach.

"I'll be back you for, snack," he muttered. I watched in frustration as the appendage regrew.

"Run," I warned in broken whisper to Bray. "Run!"

She chuckled, not moving except to widen her stance and raise her gun. Her aim proved true, with several bullets hitting the Fae tree with force. The attack slowed the Fae's lumbering progress, as he now dragged a limb behind, but still he moved forward with a wicked laugh.

Dammit. I was going to have to get up. Hands poised above the thick and ancient onyx wood, I pulled myself up, the wood splintering into my wound, my breathing labored. With arm muscles locked up in refusal to let myself drop, I heaved again. A coldness seeped from my middle, having nothing to do with blood loss, and I leaned into the pain, breathing through the wound and the agony I was causing myself. The abuse felt somehow familiar, but if my eye throbbed, it was far down on my list of current ailments.

Arms trembling, I pulled a third, fourth, and fifth time, until there was no more room to pull up. My feet gingerly found purchase on the ground, and I knew that forward motion would be painful, backward motion as well. Before allowing myself to think too closely on either, I flipped myself backwards. The searing pain made my landing sloppy, as I crashed onto a hip before pushing up again, pressing a hand against the giant hole in my stomach.

Bray's enraged scream spurred me up and into movement, sliding as I turned another corner, real or glamoured I wasn't sure. Armed with knives in each hand, Bray sliced and diced the sharpened limbs attempting to impale her.

The tree Fae had grown, considerably, as my off-centered balance sent me into the sharp corner of the alleyway. I didn't repeat my previous mistake of pouncing on his back. Instead, I slammed a kick directly between his legs.

The face that turned to scowl at me didn't hold a hint of pain.

"Just a minute, Fae Hunter, I have unfinished business with my snack," he rumbled.

"Your eyesight fails you," I hissed. Twin bursts of pain turned my vision black, leaving only the sensation of being airborne, before my back hit the stone wall with impressive force.

I cried out, feeling arm-branches impale my shoulders. Forcing my eyes to open through the mind-numbing pain, I looked directly into the leaning mouth, impressively adorned with jagged rocks. That wouldn't feel pleasant.

"I assure you," the tree warned, blowing foul breath upon me, "I never fail."

My breathing was labored, and moving my arms beyond painful as I felt the muscles contract around the wooden barbs. Landing my hands on the sticks protruding out of me, I released a brief whimper of anguish. "There's a first time for everything," I huffed out, and then pulled.

An essence flowed into me. Soul energy, raw and destructive, and I laughed in delight. The air around us cracked, growing brighter by the moment, blinding me with a heat I didn't so much feel as relish. My stomach healed, my shoulders no longer throbbed. My eyes opened to see my hands holding onto the empty husk of what once was a fearsome foe.

I tilted my head. "Does this count as his head intact?" I asked, looking to Bray, who still stood with guns at the ready in the alleyway, the real one.

Blood tripped down her temple as she limped toward me. I held out the husk of the Fae.

She swallowed, looking back at me strangely before holstering her guns.

Without a thought, I touched her temple, sending healing energy into it.

"Well, does it? I'd much prefer an apartment where you are staying, versus the rat-infested hovel I am currently forced into."

Bray nodded, looking back and forth between the husk and me.

"You fed?" she asked hoarsely.

"I believe I did. Can I heal your ankle?" I asked.

She nodded and I crouched down, touching the bruising flesh.

"How do you do that?" she asked, slowly standing to her full height.

"Do what?" I asked of her as we walked toward the car.

"Um ... uh ... Eat?" she finally settled on.

"I am not entirely sure. I just felt warmth. I think I need to be touching the being profusely, which is why I needed to be entered by it." I laughed, "I think I made another joke."

Bray chuckled, taking off her jacket to wrap the husk. "You did. And I'm still not explaining it."

"Tragic, I feel I am missing something epic," I smiled.

Chapter 5

"What do you mean, she ate it?" the disgruntled guard at the Council demanded, his unattractive face furrowed in disbelief.

"I ate its soul energy," I clarified to the troll-looking man.

He turned to me, his face impressively round, as was the rest of him, leveling a threatening stare. Or attempting to, anyway. Since I had just consumed a gorgeous amount of energy, I was fairly certain I could discard him without much effort.

He turned his gaze back to Bray, who explained, "It's a whole body, Fred, with a head." She waved it at him, smiling when he instinctually pulled back. "It's dead and I need to get paid."

"She ate its soul," Fred repeated.

"Energy," I clarified, "soul energy."

"What the fuck are you?" he demanded, his voice rising.

"Unknown," I shrugged.

"Unknown," he repeated, turning his beady gaze to Bray. "You took an unknown Supernatural on a job?" he demanded, leering over the counter.

Bray shrugged, examining the dirt on her nails. "Yep, Fred. Sure did." She looked up at him, her smile showing an excessive number of teeth.

"I gotta get the boss on this one, Bray. I've never seen a husk." He jerked a hand toward the dead body for emphasis.

I sighed, "Waiting is boring."

"Trust me, I know how you feel about it." Bray rubbed her temples.

I tilted my head. "The boss is exceptionally unhappy about being bothered," I informed Bray.

"Just wait until Fred tells him who is here," Bray muttered.

"Ah, the boss states he is rather fond of watching you walk away," I relayed to a groaning Bray. "That means he likes—"

Bray held up a hand, interrupting me. "I know what it means," she grumbled, cracking her neck before slamming her hands into her jacket angrily.

"Do you want me to eat him?" I whispered, brushing the collar of her jacket.

I could hear the smile in her voice when she answered, "Not today."

The door opened behind the long counter we were leaning against.

"Bray," a not unattractive man in a button-down shirt greeted her, pushing his brown frames up his nose before running a hand through his brown hair. Even his pants were a shade of brown, and his shirt, a brown plaid, I believe Sara had called the pattern.

"Wyatt," Bray clipped out his name.

"A husk, huh?" he asked, using a pen to shift the corpse in question.

"Yep," Bray clipped again.

"And you did this?" Wyatt swung his brown gaze toward me.

My own gaze narrowed as something dark and primal kicked around my skull, a warning of sorts that I didn't understand.

"Yep," I followed Bray's lead.

"To eat?" Wyatt clarified.

"Yep," Bray and I answered together.

"Huh." Wyatt looked over the remains once more. "Pay them, Fred, can't complain that a rogue Supernatural is off the streets. Especially one as nasty as this Fae, eating kids who climbed his branches." Wyatt shuddered before smiling. My back stiffened, claws attempting to loosen.

"You ladies stay safe out there," he finished, tipping his head, eyes lingering over me before he left.

"I can't believe I actually have to pay you two bitches for this," Fred complained.

"Language, Fred," Bray chided with a winning grin. "Can't be ruining our professional relationship and all," she added with a toothy smile. "Plus, we'd love another high hitter."

Fred grunted, "Why, she still hungry?"

I grinned, pushing my fangs down. "Famished."

...

In the car, after a stop at what was called a bank, not a treasury, guarded by stern-looking employees and not heavily armed soldiers, Bray counted out my share onto a plastic card.

"Do you think this is enough to acquire accommodations at your residence?" I asked, thumbing the thick plastic card that Bray had insisted I get.

"Yes, but you won't have anything left for a bed or food," Bray cautioned, started the vehicle.

I shrugged. "Do you hunt like this often? I don't feel the need for sustenance after draining the dryad."

"Dryad?" Bray questioned.

I nodded, tucking the card into my pocket. "Yes, the tree Fae."

She steered us out of the parking lot and into the street in the early morning hours. "How did you know it's called that?"

Her questioned carried weight, yet her voice and posture suggested differently.

"I don't know," I answered honestly. She nodded once. "You don't believe me," I complained. It was a statement.

On a long exhale, she offered only, "Don't take it personally. I don't trust many."

I nodded. "I can understand that."

"How?" she scoffed. "You can't remember last week." Her voice carried a hint of annoyance.

I wasn't willing to share with her that while I may be spelled at the moment, part of me was fighting to break free. I let my silence serve as my answer instead. As she had said, trust is reserved for the select few.

...

Bray dropped me off with a promise to be back tomorrow, after she had done research on the new target for me to eat, which would be provided by Fred through something called email. I didn't question it, understanding so little as I did.

Instead, I sat in front of the black box, watching my reflection, hoping to catch a glimpse of the Fae I was before.

...

Eventually, darkness descended, and I moved from the stained couch to the rusted platform outside the only working window.

The stars are wrong.

I jerked, looking for a voice and finding none, but I had to agree. I returned my gaze to the inky sky, dismally overpowered by the lights below.

The stars were wrong.

Eventually I made my way inside to sleep.

"Everything is so bright, sister," my brother whispered.

"Keep your eyes ahead, at the stained glass. It's the darkest point," I whispered back, also straining against my watering eyes.

My little brother nodded, his golden curls slipping out from his gold and jeweled crown, which matched my own. Already, my neck muscles strained, and a trail of sweat was beading between my shoulders.

"It's going to be okay," he whispered to me, his hand itching to hold mine. But Father had made it clear we were to stand apart and not touch.

"You will show no weakness," he had bellowed at us, hardly restraining a slap against us both. Yet with the wedding to his fifth or sixth bride (I was losing track), he couldn't risk us looking anything less than perfect.

I woke with a start, sunlight streaming through the broken shades. Sitting up, I hung my arms around my knees, shifting the strained and worn blankets around my naked form.

I could see my brother's face. The blond curls, the worried cerulean blue gaze, the smattering of freckles across his nose. I searched my memory for my own face, finding nothing but pain behind my eye. And my Father's face? I didn't even attempt to recall his.

Chapter 6

Bray arrived with others in tow. I heard their voices drifting up from their vehicles, muttering about tonight's job and the "crazy bitch" to be used as bait. Assuming that comment referred to me, I walked down to the front of the dilapidated building I unfortunately occupied. As they parked their vehicles, I stood on the broken-down black chunks of rock, called a parking lot, watching another sunset and feeling the overpowering wrongness of this world.

Bray came to stand next to me, both with our arms crossed as we watched the numerous vehicles and the meaningless activities their occupants partook in, clumped together like prey easily picked off. Bray offered a grunt of acknowledgement when Zander yelled for her, out of a vehicle she called a van.

Zander's espresso gaze never left my own as he waited for her, standing outside the van's open doors. I don't think I imagined the slamming of it when she entered, either.

Interesting. I tilted my head, trying and failing to use my Fae hearing. I shrugged. It truly didn't matter what they were discussing, as long as I was paid and fed tonight. Although I was curious how they had found a ward to block my hearing.

I turned my attention to the other white vans, their occupants not bothering to conceal their activities from me. Small wires ran over their ears, as they repeated "testing" over and over again.

Zander opened the van door and stomped toward me, brown brows drawn and a scowl on his otherwise handsome face. He thrust forward a small rectangular device, similar to the black box on the wall I disliked so.

"Phone," he clipped out.

"No," I clipped back, feeling that darkness in me seeping out. I welcomed it, as an old and familiar friend amidst this chaos.

He sighed. "We need a way to keep in contact tonight. This hit is far more complicated than the grab-and-bag last night."

I raised one caramel eyebrow. "Is there a joke in that?"

Confusion colored his face. "Joke? In the phone?"

Bray snatched the device from him, quickly scanning through images I didn't pretend to understand, faster than I was even able to read.

"Swipe up and press my face to call me," she informed me briskly.

"Why do I need the black box to call you? You are right here," I questioned.

"Jeez, you weren't kidding about her knowledge base," Zander muttered.

"I'm not. Someone took her from Faery and dropped her here," Bray muttered, watching me repeat the action.

She held her own phone up as it buzzed, before pressing a green button.

"See? Now we can talk from miles apart." Bray ended the call by pressing a red button.

"Why would we be miles apart?"

"We'll meet you at the club, Zander. I gotta get Andy changed." Bray pushed me toward my building, and I noted the bag over her shoulder.

"What's wrong with my attire?" I questioned her. "And why are you pushing me?" I demanded, removing her hands from my person.

"Are they gone?" she mouthed to me.

Tilting my head, I heard the closing of doors, followed by the revving of engines. "Yes, unless they have my hearing, we are safe."

She smiled, pressing buttons on the elevator.

"Something's off tonight," she began, waving away the question I was about to ask. "Something about tonight's grab doesn't make sense."

Once off the elevator, Bray moved quickly to my door, turning to me and waiting.

"What are you waiting for?" I asked her.

"You to unlock it?" she snapped, before trying the door and heavily rolling her eyes.

"Andy, you have to lock the door." She began unpacking the bag on the yellowed kitchen counter.

"Why?" I huffed, watching the items she moved around with distrust.

"Because bad people will take things from you." She unpacked a black silky dress, shaking out the slinky material.

"I have nothing," I pointed out.

"Then they'll hurt you," she tossed the dress, undergarments, and shoes at me.

"I'll eat them," I answered with a shrug.

"Whatever, just go put those on. You're the bait tonight. Please tell me you know what that word means."

"I do," I answered her, "but I don't understand how this dress works."

Bray shook her head and tried to explain it, but eventually ended up having to properly dress me.

"How am I supposed to be the lure?" I asked her, sitting still while she painted my lips and eyes.

"He likes pretty girls." There was a tightness in her throat, one I knew.

"Is this your kill?" I asked of her.

"No," she shook her head, black hair falling over her blue gaze and into her large, porcelain heart-shaped face. "Not this monster, at least."

I nodded. "How will I know if he's the right one?"

Pulling out her phone, she showed me a picture.

"He is handsome. I'd like to eat his face." My grin showed all my teeth and Bray chuckled, momentarily breaking her free from the dismal spell of memories.

"I'm still not explaining it," she insisted with a shake of her head. She ejected the ammunition from her gun before re-stowing it under her jacket, then double checked the knives in her boots. Rattled. She was rattled.

"What support does Zander lend to this? Perhaps he will explain it?" I grinned, teasing her, trying to keep her mind there in the present. The action felt familiar.

She outright laughed. "Please, *please* let me be there when you ask him to explain it. And I'm not sure. Zander and his team were notified when we took this case."

"Your tone suggests you don't believe that," I stated, holding up the odd shaped footwear.

"Sit," she commanded me onto the brown, discolored couch. "You read a lot by tone, you sure that's not another power of yours?"

"I don't know," I answered honestly.

"But you have a hunch," she expanded.

"I think there was a time when I had to be able to read tone, expression, body language, all of it to stay alive," I confessed, still refusing to admit to the dream memories or meet her gaze.

Bray secured the straps to my ankle. "To survive?" she asked softly.

I nodded, "I find that Liz sets off all my alarms to stay alive." I did meet her gaze then, wondering if she felt the same.

"I get that," Bray stated softly. "Let's keep this between us. Now, can you sense other Fae?"

"Yes, can't you? Oh right, half-breed."

"Are you trying to insult me?" Bray asked, exasperated. "I'm attempting to help you," she ground out.

"You are willing to use me as a lure for a deadly Fae, so define how you are trying to help me?"

Bray's lips pressed into a thin, annoyed line. She tossed a golden necklace to me. "This will protect you from being sensed by the other Fae."

I nodded, picking up the charm, the delicate symbol causing a throbbing in my left eye. I didn't sense a warning, so I slipped it on. "Where do I keep the small black box at?"

"Phone, Andy, it's a phone."

"Same question, where?"

...

Bray dropped me off a block from the bar, with instructions to follow the crowd. Other women, perhaps girls, sauntered up in the same uncomfortable shoes and limited clothing I was wearing. Few offered smiles, but they smelled of excitement. I looked upon the sea of human flesh, marveling at the ingenuity of this "den of sin," as Bray had called it. Willing victims being delivered right to the door of hungry Fae. It reminded me of the takeout Liz had ordered, and I chuckled to myself at the thought.

Although I did wonder, how did the Fae manage to keep their presence a secret? Certainly, such activity would raise questions? Hmm, perhaps the answer would lie inside.

The best places to hide are in plain sight.

I blinked, realizing that I was still an excessive distance from the entrance, in a massive holding area. Holding the clutch Bray had given to me for the black box, I turned to the brunette in a glittery dress in front of me.

"What is this?" I questioned.

"The line to get in. Getting into Wing can take hours," she added, leaning closer, smelling of inebriation. "Sometimes the owner will come out and hand select the girls they want." She giggled and smiled. My brow furrowed.

"You should leave this place," I warned her softly. Such softness was not for the Fae.

"Bitch," she snarled at me.

I shrugged, "End your life as your see fit."

I knew one thing, I was not waiting in that fucking line, which crowed the entire walkway. I forced myself into the street, vehicles swerving around me in the short black dress, my shoes clacking irritatingly. I made it to the ornate entrance, with doors high and wide enough to accommodate a troll. Hmm, the size of trolls ... an interesting memory to have return.

A Fae in a black suit with matching black glasses looked me over, a forked tongue peeking out to test my flavor. He guarded the half of the doorway with no line.

"I require entrance," I demanded of him.

He pulled down the glasses to look me over, revealing slitted pupils. "What are you, pretty?"

"Impatient," I returned, tapping my foot.

He circled me slowly, drawing his fingers over my exposed shoulder, back and collar bones. He rubbed the fingers that had touched me together. "You, you are trouble."

I smiled at him, taking a step closer. "Care to test the theory?" I whispered.

His snake like tongue peeked out again, a rumble in this throat the only affirmative answer I needed.

"Raul," another suited Fae called out from inside the doors, "just let her in, you can play with her later."

Raul nodded, slipping his glasses back up and slapping my ass as I entered. I wasn't entirely certain how I felt about that gesture.

My senses were overwhelmed. I didn't know if I wanted to puke or run screaming from the thick throng of bodies. The smells were enticing and alluring, but the music and flashing lights grated upon my temples, gradually settling into a painful throb.

Pinching the bridge of my nose, I struggled not to give in to the desire to drain all those who dared brush against me.

An unwanted arm snaked around my stomach. "Come dance with me, pretty girl," a voice whispered into my ear.

Darkness washed over me, cold seeping from my middle, as his hand attached to my hip and then roved up to my shoulder, grazing my breast on its way there. I was going to eat him, fucking literally snap off and devour one finger at a time while he watched. I may even force him to eat one himself.

My mouth opened to do such damage, the crowd and Bray's hunt be damned.

"Whoa, whoa, whoa there," said a voice drifting out of the darkness. A man with golden eyes, matching the picture Bray had shown me, gallantly shoved the man off me. "She doesn't want that, asshole," he snarled. "Get gone."

I didn't turn to see the man in question flee, because the energy washing over me from my golden-eyed prey had me questioning if I also should escape. Seeing the indecision in my emerald gaze, he quickly turned on the allure.

I didn't smile back, still uncertain while he held out a hand. Certainly, that entire display had been scripted. But prey was prey, and I consented, slipping my hand into his own. Expertly, in a move I was certain he had done hundreds of time for it to be that flawless and perfected, he tucked my hand into the crook of his arm, his digits caressing my own.

We weaved through the crowds and up a hidden stairwell, complete with its own Fae guard. The alcove we arrived at oversaw all of the floors below, placing the Fae literally on top a delicious feast of human flesh, either to enjoy or devour, which one remained unknown. I suspected both happened.

He sat us down at a dark bar of highly polished wood, turning to capture my hand once again with a wide smile.

"Can I buy you a drink?" he rumbled out, his thumb rubbing circles over my pulse. He was worming his way through my barriers; at my nod, he barked an order at the bartender. This space didn't have my senses going into overdrive. Certainly, I could still smell the humans, but it wasn't overpowering, nor was the music too loud to against my ears.

The bartender delivered our drinks with a nod, his silver hair and clear blue eyes reminding me painfully of a missing memory. I took a long sip of the beverage in front of me.

"Whoa, easy there," my companion chuckled. "What's your name?" he asked, releasing me to sip his own amber liquid from a short glass.

"Andy," I answered, tucking a strand of honey blond hair behind my ear.

"Andy," he rolled my name over his tongue. "It's a pleasure to meet you, I'm Cameron." He paused as though the name was supposed to mean something.

I smiled and leaned closer. "Wow," I breathed onto him, "your eyes are alluring." It was not my best attempt to get the male to take me home, but I didn't think calling him a pretty girl would earn me any favors. I blinked my painted gaze at him before returning to my drink, pulling several long sips.

Cameron appeared to be switching seduction tactics. I hoped he hurried up, as I was still intrigued by the doorman, and I could always eat. I chuckled to myself.

"Tell me about yourself, Andy," he inquired, laying on the allure.

I breathed it in deeply. "I can't say there's much to tell." The bartender refilled my glass and I smiled my thanks before drinking more.

He raised a mahogany eyebrow. "Sounds to me like there's a story there."

"It's a very short one," I advised, turning my full attention to him.

He shrugged, smiling again. "Short or long, I have time."

"I woke up in a hospital and couldn't remember anything, not even my name," I confessed.

"And they let you out, just like that?" Cameron questioned, raising a dark, well-groomed eyebrow.

"No, freedom always comes with constraints," I quoted—but who was I quoting? A dull throbbing began behind my left eye and I took another long drink, hoping to quell the unwelcome sensations.

"That doesn't sound like freedom," Cameron answered, pulling another drink to his lips, watching the thrall he had me in as I watched his lips capture the liquid. His throat work it down into him.

No, it didn't sound like freedom, but I failed to see the need to explain the finer details to him. Hopefully, I'd be sucking his soul dry before the next sun rose. I was beginning not to enjoy the sensations he was creating.

"What brings you to Wing?" Cameron asked, not quite willing to let the conversation lull, dropping his drink to the polished counter.

"The food," I said with a secretive chuckle, not expecting him to also laugh. He ducked his head, his unnervingly warm gaze swinging to the bartender for a moment. The break in constant eye contact was welcome and I blinked several times, certain he had used his own lure on me.

"Come with me." He waved me up with a smattering of money on the bar.

Bringing my drink to my lips, I drained it before shrugging. "Why not?" I muttered.

Cameron breezed through the club and the patrons parted to allow his exit. A dull throbbing began behind my left eye again; I had seen this before. The throbbing turned into sharply pointed pain and I exhaled a breath, turning my thoughts away from what my spelled mind hid. The night air kissed my skin in the revealing dress, and I spied the moon partially hidden behind the clouds.

"Lovely evening," he smiled, lacing our arms together, his jacket-clad arm rubbing against my own upper arm as he carefully guided my hand to his uncovered wrist.

Lust pooled inside of me at the contact with his skin. I let out a groan.

With his other hand he patted my arm, leading the way to a vehicle the color of blood, with a midnight interior. He paused for effect and I looked at him, unimpressed.

"Cars aren't your thing?" he grumbled, disappointment wafting off his pouty guise.

I shrugged, "They take you place to place, but it's not my favorite way to travel."

He sent a sidelong look at me. "What is?"

"Can't say I remember," I answered honestly. He scoffed.

"You're playing this 'can't remember' bit a little hard," he chided me.

"One would think," I agreed.

A short and speedy trip later, we arrived at a square building and true to my other experiences on Earth, the exterior left me feeling bereft. "Why are the structures here so disgusting?" I grunted.

"It's better on the inside, Princess." Cameron placed a hand on the small of my back, guiding me in.

"I certainly hope so," I answered, disgruntled.

Thick red fabric draped overhead, inky black fabric covered the walls, tables were polished until gleaming, and the people … well, let's just say I understood all the jokes Bray wouldn't explain.

"This is wonderful," I muttered, looking up at the chandelier. Gold jewelry adorned the server who deposited a glass in my hand, and little else.

"Just lovely," I sighed, watching her walk away.

"Come," Cameron said, giving my hand a tug, causing me to spill my drink. "I'll show you the food," he chuckled darkly. He pulled me quickly behind him and I scowled at his back. I supposed this scene would frighten a human, which I was supposed to be playing at. I was doing a poor job.

…

Up into the highest levels we went, where, as Cameron said, we'd find the most expensive meals.

The jewel-encrusted golden elevator saw my temper flaring. Cameron had stopped all attempts to allure or keep me compliant, and it just annoyed me that getting fed was taking so damn long.

The elevator doors opened onto a long hallway of matching doors, and now I was annoyed at the throbbing behind my eye.

He opened the third door down on the left, and shoved me in. I stumbled, turning around to glare at him as he locked the door and pocketed the key.

"Take it easy, Princess, no one cares how loudly you scream. In fact, it's more of a competition, to see how badly you beg and plead for it all to end." He chuckled, undoing his tie before removing his jacket and shirt. Normally, such a display of finely tuned muscles would cause an exceptionally different response from me.

Currently, I just wanted to drain his fucking soul.

"This isn't going to be what you think it is, Princess," he smiled, revealing fangs.

56

I raised an eyebrow. "Do I scream now?" I asked, genuinely curious. "Or is this where you go on a diatribe about all the awful things you're going to do?" I finished off the remnants of my drink.

"Who are you?" he growled, stepping forward to rip my hair back.

I sighed, annoyed. "Your conception of foreplay is poorly executed at best," I informed him, ripping off the necklace and letting my power blast free.

"Holy shit!" He backed away quickly, confusion followed by an understanding lighting his gaze. "Is this a role play?" he asked, his eyes roving over my scantily clad body with a malicious smile. "'Cause baby, I can make all your dreams come true."

I rolled my eyes. "I find you exceptionally lacking."

He swiftly removed his pants, stroking his manhood into action. I gave thought to it. I could ride him and drain him. I had actually smiled in response to that idea, when the scream of a child ripped through the air.

He watched my interest turn to horror as I dived for the key in his discarded pants. I was not prepared for him to swallow it.

"You're not getting out of here," he taunted, his glamour beginning to fade. The bones of his face pulled taut against his skin, strips peeling back, while his arms grew thicker, with fists capable of doing immeasurable damage against the skin of a child. "The doors and walls are spelled," he laughed, and razor blades accosted my ears. "You'll never escape here."

The welcome darkness spread against my stomach, reaching my chest in a refreshing wave of clarity.

"You are a fool," I whispered, dropping the clutch, along with the drained glass. I tried to step out of the restrictive shoes as well, only to find them still attached to my ankles.

With an irritated shriek, I grew my nails, slicing through the offending material. My bent over position was apparently all the invitation Cameron needed, as he threw his now massive body weight against my own.

I regretted that position instantly, as my spine attempted to snap in half at his lunge. He rolled off and I un-bent on the floor, blasting a kick against his still dangling member.

I smiled at his high-pitched howl. I was going to make him beg by the time this was done. With a snarl, he brought down one massive, meaty hand to land against my stomach. I wheezed out a breath, not having the ability to scream, feeling bones poking into places they didn't belong.

Gasping like a fish, I sent my energy to quickly heal the damage. Cameron was becoming quite the impressive foe.

Finally, a challenge.

I smiled at the thought, jumping to a crouch, seeing Cameron lumber up.

Slow moving, but hits efficiently, the other part of my brain cataloged.

Cameron's core thickened to accommodate the growing weight of his shoulders and arms. His legs thickened as well, yet didn't expand in length, leaving him looking like an overgrown toddler. I chuckled to myself, peering at his still dangling member.

"Well, Cameron, that is a shame." I drawled the words out, keeping my gaze firmly between his legs, letting my frown deepen as my head shook in disapproval. "Unable to grow the one appendage that might actually make you useful, or at least entertaining to me."

I shook down my blond hair with a shrug, noting the flared nostrils in his pinched face. He bellowed an ear-piercing scream before charging. I widened my stance, claws at the ready for his charge. The air was electric, charged with my anticipation and the magic of his change. Time slowed as Cameron's movements, while fluid, became simple to anticipate. I moved to the left with an unhurried step, easily avoiding his outstretched arm.

Fool.

Time kicked back into gear when he crashed onto the impenetrable gold door. The metal bent outward, jewels cracking under the pressure, before he was flung back against the far wall, which promptly spat him out onto the floor.

I couldn't help the full-body laugh bubbling up from my stomach, leaving me bent over, gasping for breath.

"I—I—" I tried again to get my fit of giggles under control. "I can't believe you are being bested by a magic room." I gasped for breath again, tears running down my painted face. "A room you locked us into!!" I doubled over once more, unable to contain my glee.

His bellow rang out as he sprang for me, time slowing again as I straightened up and sidestepped, moving behind him this time to pinch his ass as he flew by.

Cameron's momentum took him into an antique washbowl, complete with a blue painted pitcher. The porcelain splintered, digging deeply into his stretched skin, with one large piece embedding itself above his eyebrow and sending blood dripping into his eyes.

A noise that pitched straight to my stomach and ended my gleeful laugh ripped through the air, the sobbing scream of a child. When Cameron came ricocheting back to me, I stood in his path. My hands digging through his thick flesh, I pinned him to the ground.

He screamed, eyes widening in shock as I shrugged above him, removing his intestines, following them up toward his stomach.

A squelch told me I had found it. I shrunk my claws, lest I puncture the stomach and had to go piece by piece. Cameron attempted to put back his missing digestive tract while I rifled through his stomach acid. No key.

Annoyance colored my gaze, and I snapped the wrist that reached for me. Cameron's cry was pathetic.

"It's as though you've never truly experienced pain before, Cameron," I smiled, licking the blood on his eyebrow before rifling though his internal organs again. "Had we more time, I'd be honored to be the one to intimately acquaint you with it."

I began shredding in my search, bending his other wrist back, followed by the expansive rib collection. Acid burned at one point, but sobbing in the next room pushed me on as I squished through the delicate tissue of his lungs. He tried to bump me off of him, raising his hips in a rapid motion I'm sure he wished was doing something for me. I ripped through his spleen.

His screaming began in earnest then, accompanied by pathetic flopping around. Such a nuisance, I groaned to myself as my fingers finally slipped against metal.

"How many stomachs do you have?" I muttered, walking to unlock the door. Tossing the door open, I moved to the room next to us, trying the same key and hoping that the Fae here were foolish and lazy enough to reuse only one variation.

The lock turned over and I breathed a sigh of relief, throwing the door open with force.

The wraith in front of me was in true form, white hair clumped together, blowing in an unseen wind, her body floating above the ground, a tattered, alabaster dress revealing large chunks of missing flesh and pearly bones. She opened her mouth to scream at me, and I'm certain it would have been an impressive display of unearthly skill, but the small form huddled in the corner had me ending playtime early.

"Are you okay?" I hunched down next to the urine-scented child.

A pale face looked up at me, hands pressed tightly against her skull, thick dark hair matted to her forehead. The coldness cut inside of me until I wasn't certain I could breathe, memories swirling against the spell, pungent and dark. I closed my eyes, willing the tears of weakness to retreat. I was no good to her sobbing from my own past.

"What is going on in here?" rumbled a dark voice. "No one fucks up Dagar's brothel!"

60

I sighed, standing up to look past the now headless banshee.

"I'm not going to lie, I was really hoping this was going to end differently," I lamented with a groan and a small head shake. "I had such high hopes—a good meal, a good fuck..." I ran my hands over my made-up face. "Oh well." My foot connected to Dagar's stomach, doubling the giant over, giving me the perfect angle to push an upper cut under his chin.

Dagar let out an impressive bellow and I smiled. "Bring it," I snipped at him as his round face grew redder, horns protruding from his skull. On a hunch, I positioned in front of the room that still housed the wailing Cameron. I had certainly made a mistake not killing him.

Dagar lowered his bull-like head, charging me. I rolled my eyes, slowing time before stepping out of the way.

He crashed into the next room, and I jumped up and down in glee before following him through, pausing to toss my purse back to the huddled figure.

"Call Bray if you want to live!" I yelled as the purse smacked her right in her shocked head. Hmmm, chances of her living might be slim with me in charge.

I sauntered over to kick Dagar in the ass while he tried to get his horns out of Cameron's flesh. I was just about to remove his pants and play with his balls when he turned and tossed me ass over elbow into the wall, the warding pushing me off and into the opposite wall with force.

"She said to call you if I wanted to live!" the girl screamed at the phone.

"Tell her I understand the eating of faces now!" I yelled at the girl.

"Did you—yes! Hurry!" the girl screamed, taking in the changes in Dagar. "Please hurry!" she begged, fresh sobs freaking free.

Eventually, I settled back onto the ground. I admired the warding Dagar had implemented, quite efficient. But those praises would wait for his next lifetime. He rushed me and I jumped, using the wall as leverage before landing on his shoulders.

"Not the direction I planned on taking this," I grunted, letting my claws spring forward and into his shoulders.

Dagar closed one massive hand around my ankle, yanking me down with a solid thud.

"Ouch," I groaned, struggling to reclaim the air that had vacated my lungs.

Dagar loomed over me, ripping my dress in two. The girl screamed. Oddly, I felt nothing.

"You bitch!" he bellowed. "No one attacks me!"

I shoved both my hands deep into the cavity of his head, and sucked the life force right out of him.

"This bitch just did."

...

I sat across the abandoned street, watching the humans file out of the square box called a warehouse, all stinking with fear, all dirty. A few had to be carried, a few too young to be without mothers.

Eventually, Zander sat next to me.

"You need to wash," he commented.

"I enjoy the blood of my enemies," I countered. "You require information," I stated.

He looked down at his black shoes. I was now adorned in an oversized shirt, found in the warehouse. "I'm just checking on you," he protested.

"You do not like me, and you do not care for the state of my mental or physical well-being. What do you want?" My voice held no emotions, only facts.

"You're making me out to be an asshole here." He ran a hand through chocolate strands.

I said nothing, since there was nothing to say.

On a long-winded sigh, he finally asked what he wanted to know. "Do you know what type of Fae Dagar was?"

I shrugged. I could probably place it if I concentrated, but I lacked the desire to do so.

"Who is Andromalius?" I countered.

His gaze widened. "No one," his quickly supplied.

"Lies," I sneered, "you do it so poorly."

"Oh, and you do it better?" he snapped.

"I don't do it at all," I informed him.

"Everyone lies," he stated.

"Unless you don't," I hissed back at him.

As we stared daggers at each other, Bray chose that moment to interrupt. "Andy, you ready to head back?"

"Did we make enough?" I asked.

"Yeah, you did," she answered.

I nodded. "Then I am satisfied to leave."

Once in her car and pulling away from the mess, I asked, "What happens to the children?"

Bray looked over at me, taking her time to answer. "Their families will be contacted. Some may have been reported as missing."

"Those who weren't?" I pushed.

"Foster care, a temporary home until they are of age," Bray supplied.

"They are expendable," I stated.

"They were treated like that," Bray agreed.

I nodded, at a loss for words to articulate what was happening inside of me. The cool indifference I had known was thawing, an inferno of rage replacing it. A rage I knew had never seen the light of day.

...

I tried to ward off sleep in the decrepit hovel, knowing the dreams it would bring, the blue eyes I refused to remember in my waking hours, now vibrantly alive while my mind wandered.

The dungeon's filth made the warehouse's decrepit conditions appear pleasant.

"Have you decided who?" a voice to my right asked.

I wanted to turn and see who it was, but instinct warned me better. It was a sick game, and one he enjoyed well. Playing God with who would live, who would live but suffer, and who would suffer but be allowed to die.

The dungeon housed a man, wasting away, hanging in chains. A child clothed in rags, but with high cheek bones and full lips. An old woman who had lost the entirety of her teeth, hunched over and hobbling around. I didn't need to look further for what he wanted.

I nodded, pointing to the small dark form of a child, around my age, with piercing blue eyes peering at me.

"How lovely," he chuckled, my shoulders hunching into myself at the sound. "I couldn't have picked a better plaything for the troops myself."

...

Pulling my legs to my chest, I rested, my sweat-covered forehead against my knees. She deserved the horrors that her long life would give her. She was lesser and subject to the wants and needs of Royalty. I had to choose her. I had to show no mercy and no care for the brutality she endured.

Wasn't she? Didn't I?

Despair and hopelessness rose inside of me, an emptiness that threatened to swallow me whole. But I found myself wishing to not remember, not any of it.

Chapter 7

The next morning, Bray dropped a box of kitchenware on the counter of my newly acquired apartment. "It's not much," she admitted as she sorted through it.

I shrugged, "It's enough." I set my limited clothing down in the master bedroom. What I was supposed to do with a second bedroom was beyond me. "It's an improvement. On the tour, the witch said there is a medical unit in the basement."

Bray nodded her head with a shrug, keeping her gaze on the futon beside me, which had come from her storage unit. "Glad she's going to a good home. Don't break her."

I chuckled. "What time does Seth get off? I'd like to break him," I laughed. "I understand the jokes now!"

Bray twirled a strand of dark hair around her finger, not impressed. "Hands off."

"Why are you claiming him?" I asked with honest curiosity.

"Claiming?" she questioned.

I nodded, dumping out the clothing while vaguely remembering her saying something about hanging it. I wasn't sure why I should kill my clothes.

"What does 'claiming' involve, exactly?" she asked uncertainly, leading me into the closet and showing me how to use hangers.

"Fucking and biting." I waggled my eyebrows.

"Oh shit, that's not a visual I'll be easily getting rid of," Bray moaned, snapping her eyes shut and pinching the bridge of her nose. She shook her head, presumably to make an attempt. "Seth and I..." She looked to the heavens for inspiration on how to proceed, before shrugging and returning her attention to me. "We work cases together, occasionally. He wishes there was more between us."

"And you don't?" I asked. I certainly wished there was more between Seth and me—or perhaps less was the proper verbiage.

Bray shrugged. "He's a shifter, a Supernatural of Earth, with a pack and responsibilities. I'm a half-Fae, not wholly of Earth, who hunts down rogue Fae. How would that work?" she asked, pinning me with her blue eyes, sincere in her inquiry.

I didn't see why it wouldn't "work." I thought of asking if her genitals were mutilated, but her eyes steered me away from that line of questioning. Instead I went with, "Being scared of how it would work is a poor reason not to try making it work. Perhaps it won't," I shrugged. "What have you lost besides time?"

Bray crossed her arms, "I don't want to be hurt," she painfully confessed.

"Then you risk losing far more than a mate," I informed her. "Life is bloody, Bray, it requires our pain to build our joy."

Her dark brow drew down. "That's rather deep for you."

"Agreed. Let's pretend it never happened," I teased with a smile.

...

Night had fallen, and I found myself content, sitting on the roof of the U-shaped building. Several signs warned that I wasn't to be out here. I dared someone to complain. Besides, the doors were open.

The missing memories still plagued me, but in this moment, I had done good. I had freed the weak, dispensed justice, and put my considerable skills to use.

Eventually, I retired alone to the futon, which seemed like a waste. Maybe Seth had a friend.

"She's awful!" my mother screamed. "I don't want her!"

Something crashed close to my head, and I burrowed deeper into the corner I found my small form in.

"She's your daughter, Aneja," another voice reprimanded.

"She's HIS daughter, the spawn of true evil, and she is going to destroy us all!" My mother threw another vase, this one landing against my small head.

"Enough, Aneja. The only one destroying things is you."

I jerked awake from the memory, my heart aching.

After my fitful night, I was seriously questioning my intelligence in agreeing to "go for a run" in the wilderness park.

"I fail to see the import of this activity," I huffed, climbing another hill.

Bray smiled, which in itself seemed insane. "We have to stay in shape, to catch the bad guys, which gets us paid."

"Are they always guys?" I questioned.

She shook her ebony hair, filled with perspiration that matched my own blond ponytail, as she had called it. "Females are often the worst," she confided.

"Why?" I asked, truly wondering. From the night's reemergent memories, her claim held truth. Was it because females were the nurturers of the species, so when they failed to do so the pain was twofold?

Bray shrugged, jumping over a downed tree. "I don't know," she huffed.

We ran around the bend, me lost to my own thoughts, only to skid to a stop at the massive tree downed in our path.

"What the actual fuck? Like this loop isn't challenging enough," Bray grumbled under her breath as she looked for options. Turning around did not seem like a bad choice to me.

"Bray," I warned softly. She stopped, pinning me with annoyed blue eyes.

"What?" she snapped.

I scanned the area, listening with my advanced hearing. "Nothing," I concluded with a shake of my head.

The log consumed the trail, branches spreading over and out, covering the dirt path with thin, needle-like leaves.

"Under or around?" Bray debated out loud.

I looked at the around prospect, thinking it did seem to be the better choice, even if the rocky outcroppings appeared unsteady. Turning my attention back to Bray, I found her attempting under, pushing the thinner branches out of her way and complaining the entire time.

With a sigh of annoyance, I followed her through.

...

Darkness assaulted us, a perfectly pitched blackness. Instinct kicked in and I grabbed Bray, dragging her to the ground.

"What the fuck?" she hissed.

I uttered no words, my senses reaching out, attempting to track the untraceable.

"Andy—" I silenced her with a hand over her mouth, certain her sapphire gaze would be furious for the insult.

A scattering behind had us both turning our attention there. Bray got onboard with being silent, and I removed my hand. The screaming of my legs from previous use was forgotten as I kept myself crouched. Moving would have been preferable, but instinct told me to stay still.

Bray, however, was of no such opinion, and began to crawl back the way she thought we had come. Not her best decision. I could keep her safe, but using her as a distraction was the far superior idea. Stillness seeped into my bones, my gaze riveted to Bray and the surrounding darkness. Danger was coming from that direction.

Leave her, a voice whispered. *She's not waiting for you.*

Leave Bray? The only friend I had? Could I do that? Could I leave her here, to die? The voice was correct, she wasn't waiting for me, but I had no doubt that she also wouldn't leave me here.

I dismissed the idea, renewing my gaze at Bray as she stumbled in the dark.

The stench of death wafted over my shoulder, carried by warm breath, entirely too close to me. Slowly, I turned to look at the mouth that had produced it: blackened, crooked teeth made to rend flesh from bone, housed in purple lips that smiled grotesquely. Thick hair, greasy and unkempt, hung heavily on each side.

Without thought, I slammed my forehead against her nose, and found myself rolling away. A rak, a fucking rak, I hissed at myself, irritated. I should have sensed it, should have known it.

I scrambled through the darkness. Dead bodies littered the ground, and I flung them around recklessly in my hasty search.

Scattering on her eight legs, the half-spider, half-woman plowed into me. I took the hit, feeling her pincers grind into my hip. Shifting my body toward the wall of darkness she had pinned me on, I slammed my shoulder into her chin.

Her roar was the stuff of nightmares. Down again I went, this time tossing discarded carcasses at her to gain myself time.

Her roar turned into a screech, and I heard Bray's own scream of horror leave her mouth.

Fuck. The rak turned, a smile replacing her scowl as she searched out the additional prey in her lair. "Fight her, Bray!" I screamed, tossing half-consumed bodies, shaking out clothing as I went. I overturned an altar, scattering candles over the inky ground.

"How the fuck do I fight Spider Woman?" Bray screamed.

"Don't you have a weapon on you?" I demanded, stopping my search, my hands dripping with bodily fluids. "Don't kill her—"

Bray ducked before I heard her grunting. "But she's trying to kill *me*!" she screeched back.

"Don't let her, not until I find the gem!" I bellowed back.

Reaching the rak's rotted sleeping mat, I ripped the damn thing into two, watching as the red gem fell out. I lunged for it. No larger than my thumb, it had to be powerful in construction to cage a rak. I pinched down, letting my magic flow into the blood-red gem.

A resounding boom sent us all flying back to reality. Landing flat on my back, I fought to sit up, the echoes ruining my hearing for the moment and knocking the wind from me. Bray sprawled next to me on the trail, blood seeping from a gash on her forearm.

On the tree crouched the rak, face poised to the sunshine, arms extended out wide.

"Ouch," Bray groaned.

The rak's attention moved to us. "Thank you," she growled over her thick back teeth.

"Anytime," I grunted, lying back down. In a wind of freedom, she was gone.

"What the fuck was that?" Bray whispered at me.

"I think that was attempt number two on your life," I answered.

"Why did you free it? It's going to kill others," she hissed in annoyance, pushing to an elbow.

"She will, but it will be those responsible for capturing her," I shrugged. "Raks are docile by nature, unless captured. When confined, she slowly starves, so when fresh meat wanders by, or is lured into her lair, she kills without question," I finished, slowly pushing to my feet.

"How do you just know this stuff?" she asked as I offered her a hand up. "It took me years of studying to learn a fraction of what you know, and what?" she asked, brushing herself off. "Now these fucked up, elite and mysterious Fae are making an appearance to kill me?"

"Think how knowledgeable you'll be if you keep surviving these death attempts," I offered.

Bray wheeled, her chest puffing, her gaze screaming her irritation. "Andy—" She shook her head. "Forget it, I don't even know where to begin on that one. My pride is hurt and my ability to defend myself is being tested and damn near broken. I don't fucking like this, and I want it to end."

I shrugged, worry eating at me for the voices I was hearing.

Bray looked up, shading her eyes against the sun. "It's setting?" she questioned. "It was morning when we got here."

"Time moves differently in other realms," I shrugged. "And I need a shower." I plucked a finger bone from my pony tail.

We decided to walk back to the car, Bray silent and in deep thought.

Hopefully, she was working out who was trying to kill her ass, because they clearly had resources and access to her schedule.

The ride back was silent, although we did enjoy the sunset.

Before we departed the car, Bray looked at me intently. Sensing she was about to speak, I paused mid door opening.

"Are you going to tell anyone about this?" she wondered.

"And who exactly do I speak to, other than you?"

"Zander and Liz," her answer came quickly.

"It is your business, Bray. I won't get involved." The words came easily enough that I wondered if I had used them before.

She nodded once.

"Any work for tonight?" I asked as we reached the front door.

She shook her head, blasting by Seth at the desk without looking at him. I let her go, sensing she needed her space.

"What happened, y'all get lost?" Seth asked.

"Actually, we did," I confirmed.

"Huh," he nodded as I went to the left, finding my stairwell access.

...

Seth was gone by the time I had showered and changed. I asked the night guard for directions to procure food.

"There's an excellent Italian joint just three blocks over, serves a mean meatball," the sandy-haired shifter conveyed, looking down as he wrote out directions.

"What makes a meatball mean?" I asked.

He paused, flashing dimples. "Uh, you're teasing me?" he laughed.

I shook my head.

"Tasty, the meatballs are tasty. It's just another way to say it. Are you sure you don't want to get your phone?" he asked, worry creasing his forehead.

I shook my head. "Thank you."

"Yeah, anything ... uh, anytime," he muttered.

I smiled. "Define anything," I teased.

He chuckled, whistling low. "Anything," he repeated with a wink.

I hoped he would still be working after I found traditional nourishment. I wasn't certain I required food, the tangible kind and not just soul energy, but I did wish to see more of the city, even if my instincts screamed that I wouldn't be here long.

The directions led to me a restaurant with outdoor dining under a red canopy. The food, as the door attendant had promised, was delicious. I ate until my stomach was full but still felt hungry, just not for food.

I was chewing on my straw, debating finding a rogue Fae to eat—assuming I could define what rogue was—when Zander walked by.

I stilled myself, willing the night to swallow me whole. Interesting, it was glamour but not quite. I didn't waste time analyzing it. Having already paid my bill with the plastic card Bray had supplied, I slipped from my seat, easily swinging my jeans-clad body over the low iron divider.

I hissed, looking down at the iron burn on my hand. Right, Fae and iron ... should have known that. Closing the injured appendage, I followed behind Zander, using all my considerable skills to stay hidden in the shadows. He glanced back once when I was tucked into a patch of pure darkness with a rancid smell, his brow furrowed, lips drawn tightly. I was learning that upset, annoyed, or irritated was his usual disposition.

Through the rundown and dilapidated buildings he wove, deeper, until the businesses and massive stone buildings gave way to equally dilapidated homes. Roofs were caved in, wooden beams exposed in the rotting interiors. Black paint marred the few unbroken windows; most had already been shattered.

What was Zander doing here?

I tucked myself into a home when another shadow emerged ahead. "Did you walk the entire way here?" Liz scolded.

74

"It felt like I was being followed. I was being smart. What are you wearing?" he demanded disapprovingly. I risked being seen to glimpse what he was speaking of.

Liz wore a golden gown of silk and a matching crown of golden leaves, her glasses gone and her lips ruby red. The material swirled around her legs, revealing slits up her thighs.

"We are the ruling body here. It's important we convey that to those coming through."

Zander grunted. "Who's coming through tonight?" he asked despondently.

"Someone worth the effort to impress." Liz snapped her fingers, and Zander's jeans and jacket were replaced by leather breeches, boots, and a golden tunic with blue stitching.

He sighed, "Summer Court colors, really? Tempting fate, don't you think?"

"We once belonged to Summer Court," Liz reminded him, moving into a particularly disgusting home.

"We did, and now we have no Court," Zander snarled low.

"Which is why we are here, building our own Courts," Liz reminded him as she brushed lint from her dress. Though their voices were muffled in the house, I could still hear perfectly.

"We lose over half of the Fae we bring over; I don't think we are building anything very successfully," he confessed miserably.

"It's not our job to protect everyone," Liz smugly stated, and I found myself thinking I had said those exact words.

"You sound like a spoiled Princess we once knew," Zander muttered.

"Maybe she knew something we didn't," Liz mused.

"What? How to torture or remove magic by sex?" Zander snipped.

"I told you not to sleep with the bitch," Liz smugly reminded. "Things were far better when you were in my bed."

Zander sighed. "I remember, and you've frequently reminded me. Leave your jealously for my infatuation with Andromalius in the past, where it belongs."

Liz huffed, "Too bad you couldn't seduce her back into your bed. Regaining your powers over the dead would definitely help our cause."

"I don't understand why you constantly need to bring this back up," Zander snapped.

"Perhaps if you let me teach you," Liz crooned. "We only share a father," she whispered. "Tell me you don't remember all the enjoyable things we did before we leaned that."

Ewwww. Was she implying what I thought she was implying?

"Enough, I am tired. We have an entire race to save from the insanity of the Summer King," Zander complained. "Let's open the damn portal."

A snapping of fingers was met with truck doors opening. I peeked out from my hiding spot, seeing two tall humans dragging a third between them.

A sacrifice. They don't have the natural power to open portals.

"Do I?" I whispered softly.

The voice inside my head scoffed, *We have the power to ruin kingdoms.*

I heard the scuffle before the human's throat was slit and the chanting began. Idly, I wondered if I was supposed to have saved said human.

The combined voices of Zander and Liz raised the small hairs on my neck. I wanted to get closer to see the portal opening, and whoever they thought was so important coming through. But I stayed outside, waiting for them to leave. Even if waiting was still my least favorite activity.

Patience, my voice inside counseled, and I listened.

Their voices rose and the tempo increased, the wind outside picking up and whipping around the house. I searched the street, wondering if someone, anyone would come forward to investigate the odd weather. But Liz and Zander had chosen their location well. If any inhabitants did lurk in the shadows, they knew to stay away.

A bolt of lightning struck the street, and the voices, which had risen to be heard over the wind, quieted. Electricity tingled up my arms, discharging down my spine until I shook out the residual charge their casting had caused.

A few moments of silence breathed through before I heard Liz speaking. "Welcome to Earth, realm of possibilities and safety," she falsely assured the newcomers.

"Thank you, Eliza, for opening the portal for us. In truth, I was afraid you wouldn't be able to honor our agreement and take a wild portal through, as unstable as they are. But I fear I have grave news. The Blood Kingdom has fallen to Summer Court," the woman whispered tearfully.

Silence, before Zander finally spoke. "What of Shadows?" he questioned.

"They fell before us," the speaker sadly conveyed.

"Who is left?" Zander whispered.

"Not many. We are scattered and fallen. The wrath of the Summer King is relentless and heartless." The cry of an infant disturbed them.

"The heir of the Blood Kingdom?" Liz or Eliza asked softly.

"Aye, his father died bravely defending us." More broken sobbing.

"You'll be safe here," Eliza claimed yet again.

Together with the new recruits, Liz/Eliza drove off. Zander stood alone on the sidewalk, watching the black car disappear.

Once it was out of sight, a second, matching black vehicle appeared. "Get rid of the body," Zander snapped to the two Harkers who lumbered out of it.

"Nice threads, boss," one of them tossed over his shoulder.

Zander grunted, still staring after the vanished tail lights that had carried away his sister.

Summer Court. Blood Kingdom. Was it all supposed to mean anything to me?

...

I didn't want to return to my chambers, instead wandering until I found the bar where Bray and I had killed the dryad.

The joint was loud, a raucous cacophony of voices, all competing to be heard in the small space. The tables were packed with bodies, and the bar offered no respite, with Fae bodies of its own pressed too tightly together.

Cool night air wafted in from the open doors and windows, while a band set up to play along the far wall to my left. The shifter at the bar nodded to me. "What will it be?" he asked, slinging a stained rag over his shoulder.

I tilted my head. Soda hadn't agreed with me, but I didn't get the name of the drink Cameron had ordered. So I shrugged, "I'm open."

His wide grin crinkled his eyes, and I had a hard time not smiling back. "Famous last words," he muttered.

Again I shrugged, while he mixed unknown liquids together and presented them to me in a chilled glass.

Another patron yelled from farther down, so the bartender tapped the worn wood in front of me. "Let me know how you like it," he offered distractedly as he moved down the line.

I took a tentative sip, only to have my arm jostled by the patron to my left. The growl that left me wasn't loud enough to pierce through his drunken stupor. With a turn, he muttered. "Apologies," before turning back to his companion.

"No, Andromalius is the worst," he hissed in a loud whisper, shaking his head.

"No, no, her brother Kolm is the biggest bastard in Fae, forcing us all to flee or agree to their rule of tyranny," the bearded man bellowed. "Cut down my own family while they made me watch." He took a long drink from his glass, draining it and tapping the bar for another.

"The things those monsters did to my children..." His eyes were haunted as he and his companion exchanged horror stories.

"That bitch," the lighter-haired patron began. "She enjoyed it. That," he said, tapping on the bar forcefully, "that makes her the worst. "Her smile, while she..." He couldn't finish it before taking his own long drink. "Her laugh haunts me, the joy she took in slicing apart my village. I've never seen such glee in one so evil before."

The bearded man grunted, "I'll agree with that. She does enjoy it far more than her sibling." They drank in silence, each lost to his own memories.

The woman to my other side, dark hair hanging over her face, chimed in, "You forget her love of carving into people." She flipped her hair back, and both men cringed at what she revealed.

"Hello, Darla," they muttered together, awkwardly wrapping their unwanted conversation around me.

"While you two were busy hiding and running away, I suffered under her men and her sick ways," she hissed.

The men had no rebuttal to that, hanging their heads in shared shame.

"It wouldn't have done any good," the bearded one muttered softly.

Darla scoffed, "At least you'd have died a hero's death, instead of ending up as a haunted old Fae, too afraid to live." She turned her attention to me, openly staring at her. "Like what you see?" she sneered.

"No," I answered, watching her one good eye blink. The pink, raw, crisscrossing wounds on her face wouldn't ever properly heal. They were inflicted with iron.

Tossing money on the counter, I left.

...

My walk back to the big U was haunted by a voice I was beginning to think I knew. Yet I hesitated to voice my well-founded suspicious out loud, even if I was the only one who could hear.

The Shadow Kingdom has fallen.

The Blood Kingdom has fallen.

The voice in my head was terrified.

He's coming, he's coming.

"Who?" I whispered.

The Father.

....

After a sleepless night, I headed down to Bray's, hoping she could offer something to kill. Laughter greeted me, and I debated if I was welcome. While Bray was the only member of this wretched world I'd call a friend, I wasn't one she laughed with. Maybe at, but rarely with.

I had turned to head back to my place when Seth called my name. I spun to see him sauntering down the hall.

"Hey, you coming for breakfast?" he asked eagerly.

I shook my head. "No, I don't want to interrupt."

"Nonsense." He pulled me behind him, opening the door without knocking. "Bray's mom makes the best breakfast," he announced loudly.

"Seth," an older version of Bray greeted him, kissing each cheek before turning back toward the tiny apartment kitchen. "You know it's Braelyn," she chided over her shoulder.

The one in question groaned, "It's Bray, Mom. Just Bray."

80

I peered at Bray's mother in the kitchen, clattering away. Her daughter had inherited her thick, dark hair and high cheek bones, although Bray's full lips must have come from the other half of the parental equation.

"Oh, well … hello," the woman greeted my intense stare.

"Just ignore her, Mother. Andy has brain problems," Bray quickly supplied.

"I lack my full memory," I clarified.

"See, brain problems plus issues socializing," Bray added, pulling me further into the apartment.

I didn't budge or shift my gaze. "You are full Fae," I stated.

Bray's mother stopped stirring the pot on the stove. "I am," she replied.

"And you have bred with a human?" I asked, again shocked at the notion.

She cleared her throat. "I did," she answered.

"Disgusting," I snapped, before slapping a hand over my own mouth. "Sorry, I don't know or understand why I said that." She nodded and Bray ushered me into the living rom.

"See, brain issues," Bray reiterated over her shoulder.

I shrugged. Her explanation did seem more reasonable than any I could offer.

…

"You seem uncertain, dear," Bray's mom commented as I was again staring rudely.

"I am lost," I replied. "Having my memories taken has left gaping holes in who I am … or was, or whatever."

"And you want to remember who you were?" she asked tentatively.

"More than anything," I whispered earnestly.

She nodded, opening her mouth and closing it again before finally deciding to speak. "I'm just going to say this and take it as you will. The person who judged me for having Bray and the person who apologized are two vastly different Fae. I'd caution you about retrieving those lost memories. You may not like what you find."

I nodded. "That is wise advice, thank you," I replied in earnest.

...

I had to admit, Seth wasn't wrong about the breakfast. After piling seconds onto her plate, Bray declared that she and I had work to do.

"Your mother is exceptionally kind," I said to her once we were alone and looking over cases. "How did you come to be a Fae bounty hunter?"

Bray swallowed down the food she had just shoved into her face—from her expression, painfully. "My dad was killed by a rogue Fae when my mom was pregnant." She shrugged, pushing the food around her plate. "It sparked something in me, a need for justice. The previous bounty hunters never found out who did it."

I nodded. "Have you tried to locate the guilty Fae?" I asked.

"I have—I did," she amended, watching my reaction closely.

"I hope you delivered lifetimes of punishment," I informed her somberly.

"Thanks," she grumbled around another mouthful of food, before plopping down a case. "I usually don't take kid cases, but I'm tempted to make an exception if you'll help out."

Pulling the case toward me, I nodded. "I'm hungry."

Bray laughed, "You're always hungry."

I didn't mention that I had used my magic, and therefore some of my energy, to hide myself from Zander and Eliza-Liz. Now didn't seem like the time for that, though I wasn't sure how my job performance would be affected. Not to mention that I didn't want to worry her with who "he" was and why he was coming.

Not a joke in that one.

"What is that thing?" I muttered, tilting the black and white picture. "It's drawn exceptionally poorly."

Bray looked at me over the file. "A child drew it," she sighed. "My best guess is a vampire who preys on children."

My brow furrowed at her. "But does it only feed on human children?"

"Under the age of ten," Bray expanded.

"That isn't right," I muttered. My eyes narrowed at the black and white photo of the child's drawing, as though the simple act of glaring would reveal its secrets.

"Uh, what's not right?" Bray asked, looking over my shoulder.

An unsettled sensation descended onto my chest, one tinged with the heaviness of fear.

"I need to talk to the child," I commanded.

Chapter 8

The home was elegant, situated on a sprawling estate with perfectly trimmed hedges, vines climbing the brick structure, and vivid flowers growing everywhere.

"This is where we should live," I observed. I most assuredly belonged in a place of this caliber.

Bray huffed next to me on the marble stairs, "You'll need to catch a whole lotta bad guys to get a joint this nice."

I shrugged. "If I even stay long enough," I softly admitted, running my hands over the delicate metal work.

"Why wouldn't you stay long?" Bray's voice was guarded.

I turned to her, searching for a reason that wasn't a complete lie. "I'm not sure I belong here."

She nodded, pressing the call button. "But you like it here?" she asked.

"I know nothing else, but yes, I am beginning to enjoy it here."

"Just not enough to stay," Bray wisely finished.

"I still crave what I'm missing."

The large glass door soundlessly opened to reveal a gray-haired women in a spotless white apron.

"Yes?" she asked, her accent oddly familiar.

"Hi, I'm Bray. I called earlier, we are investigating the attack on Aiden."

The woman narrowed her brown gaze, the door inching slowly closed.

"Claudette?" a voice from inside called. "Who is here?"

A blond woman in navy dress pants pulled open the door, her white blouse also perfectly spotless. She smiled, waving us in. "Please step inside, you must be the investigators, coming to find the horrid monster that attacked my son. Claudette, tea, if you please."

Claudette and I had our gazes locked, each sensing a predator, but I was in the dark as to what she was. I had no doubt that my missing memories would have filled in the blank. Instead, our eyes just exchanged barbs before she went to do as requested.

"You must be Mrs. Brandson, thank you so much for seeing us on such short notice," Bray began, stepping into the parlor and taking a seat on the burgundy floral sofa.

I perched next to her in the high-backed antique.

"Of course, we need closure," Mrs. Brandson solemnly confided to Bray, sitting on a baby blue couch and crossing her navy-clothed legs. "Aiden, poor Aiden, has had a terrible time sleeping. We've got him seeing a counselor, along with taking sleeping pills, but I'm afraid nothing is working. His father is away on business, unfortunately, and in the meantime, Aiden's created this absurd story of what really happened. The counselor said it's normal for children to assign supernatural attributes to such a painful event."

Bray nodded, "I'm so sorry to hear that. Would it be possible to speak with Aiden?"

Mrs. Brandson pursed her lips a moment. "Yes, I suppose that'll be all right. Let me go check on him."

"Thank you," Bray reassured.

Claudette appeared with the tea just as Mrs. Brandson was exiting.

"You're not welcome here," she hissed, dropping the tea onto the oak table.

"Why not?" I demanded.

Her dark gaze locked onto mine. "You're Fae," she hissed, letting loose a long, forked, purple tongue.

I raised an eyebrow at her. "True, as are you, Vitore."

She hissed again, revealing long rows of serrated teeth.

"Andy," Bray whispered.

"Relax. The lady of the home invited us, so Vitore here cannot harm us," I dismissed Bray's concern over the slobbering serpent in human form. I tilted my head at the Fae in question. "The real question is, why are you here, and do they know of your true form?"

Claudette snapped her gaping mouth shut, stepping backward until she was in the hallway. "The father has demanded protection for his child. The mother," she huffed out, smoke wafting from her human nostrils, "knows nothing."

I nodded, hearing Mrs. Brandson clicking down the stairs with another pair of shuffling feet.

"Aiden has only a few minutes between homework assignments," Mrs. Brandson announced, escorting her son down. "I told him you would be quick."

"How did you survive?" I asked, genuinely curious.

"Please excuse my partner, Aiden. Her manners are absent. We are investigating what—I mean, who—attacked you, and hoping you might be able to answer a few questions to aid us." Bray's glare in my direction was exceptionally potent. I did lack manners.

Aiden wouldn't meet my gaze. His auburn hair falling over his eyes, he shrugged.

"Did it sing to you?" I asked, scooching forward on the floral settee.

He gasped, now jerking his gaze to mine. "Maybe paralyzed you, so you couldn't move?" I continued. Again, he nodded. "Then what?"

He sputtered, looking over at his mother's disapproving gaze. "It sniffed me," he spoke, barely above a whisper, "then snarled and left." His voice shook. "Just left. I don't know if it's coming back or what!" he screeched, before running to Claudette and burying his head in her apron, sobbing.

I looked at Bray, who was unnerved by my line of questioning to say the least, then returned my attention to Aiden's terrified form. "It won't come back," I concluded.

I stood, resting my hand on Aiden's shoulder and meeting Claudette's gaze. "You are safe, Aiden," I offered, the softness of my voice surprising me. "It won't come back for you."

"But others, it will hunt others?" his soft voice wafted up to me.

I broke eye contact with the serpent protector to smile down at him. "Not when I get done with it."

....

Bray was angry.

"You knew what it was?" she asked, slamming an open palm against the steering wheel. Which, in my personal opinion, was daring, considering the dilapidated condition of the car.

"I had a hunch," I confided, buckling my seatbelt.

She cranked the vehicle to life with far too much force. "And you couldn't be bothered to fucking share?!" She had escalated to yelling.

I sighed, "I think this thing ... I think I have a history with it."

"Why?" she rapid-fired back.

"Because ... I am ..." *Afraid* wasn't a word I'd voice. "I am uncomfortable with it." That was better.

That stumped her for a moment as she pulled into the street. "You're not acting uncomfortable."

"Fear is a weakness that cannot be seen," I quoted, again not knowing who, what, or where the words came from.

Bray was silent for several moments, finally deciding on, "How do we track it?"

"We're going to summon it."

She slammed on the brakes. "We're. Going. To. WHAT?!"

I nodded, forcing myself not to wring my hands in my lap or let my pores begin to sweat.

"I'll need an animal to sacrifice, and a sacred circle set up."

Bray slowly moved the car along again, silent as she drove.

...

We arrived at a small, yellow, brick-faced shop, with a neon sign reading "Psychic."

"What is this place?" I rumbled, annoyed and seeing no value in it. There were no hints of the items I had requested.

"A friend. I think he'll be able to help us with your supply issues." She didn't meet my gaze as we got out of the vehicle.

Inside the windowless shop, a man was hunched over the counter, wearing a yellow shirt matching the obnoxious paint job outside.

He looked up as the bell above the door announced our arrival.

"Braelyn," he beamed, extending his arms as he came around the counter, losing quite a few inches in height in the process. Bray's smile widened as she awkwardly embraced the short, bald Fae.

"Hello, Lev."

"What brings you to my shop today?" Lev asked, climbing back up the stairs behind the counter.

Bray sighed. "This is going to be a weird one," she confessed, tousling her short, black strands. She drew a breath then turned, pinning me with a meaningful look.

I assumed it was my turn to explain. "We need to hunt a—" I struggled to find the right word. "I mean, I need to cast a circle, and sacrifice an animal to summon and kill a child killer."

There, that was it.

Lev's obsidian eyes blinked at me, then narrowed. "A Baubas?" he asked in disbelief.

"Yes," I confirmed.

His lips smashed together, his brows drawn disapprovingly down. "What makes you think you can summon her?" he asked, fiddling with a blue tassel pen on the counter.

I shrugged, offering no further explanation.

He nodded, "And if it responds?"

"We kill it," Bray answered.

Again, Lev just nodded, before releasing a deep sigh that had his stomach moving. "It can't be done, I've tried."

It was Bray's turn to narrow her eyes. "Explain."

Lev waved a hand, dismissing her serious tone. "I've heard it was here, preying on children, and thought if I could summon it into a well-warded circle of protection, I could kill it."

Bray crossed her leather-clad arms. "But?" she demanded, tapping her foot impatiently.

"But it can't be done." Lev threw up his hands in defeat. "I've tried hundreds of variations, and nothing works. She is a beast that cannot be summoned."

"You could have been killed, Lev!" Bray reprimanded the man who appeared to be far older than her.

I sighed heavily. "The other option is to use a child as bait," I shrugged, knowing neither of them would agree to it.

"What Fae parent is going to volunteer their child as bait?" Bray asked me.

I shrugged, pretty certain mine would.

"Can we track it?" I asked of Lev.

He shrugged, "You'd have to know someone who actually survived an attack."

Bray and I shared a look. "We do."

...

Aiden's mother was less than pleased by our second appearance in one day, and the fuss she made about getting his blood was grinding my limited patience to a pulp.

"I just don't think we can do this," she finally settled on, nodding emphatically, willing us to agree with the conclusion.

"Mrs. Brandson, taking just a few drops of his blood will possibly allow us to track the beast that attacked your son, and be certain no one suffers from it again," Bray explained again.

She shook her head again, meeting Claudette's gaze in the corner. "No, I'm sorry, I can't do it. Please just go." With that, she turned from the high-ceilinged entryway where we had made our request.

Claudette was only too happy to show us her serrated teeth when we didn't move quickly enough for her liking.

The tall iron door slammed behind us.

"Well, fuck," Bray hissed, opening the car door.

I had to agree.

"What now?" She slammed the vehicle into drive, causing it to lurch.

"We can try my blood, but I fear that will bring more problems than solutions."

"Why?" Bray demanded. "What problems?"

I sighed, annoyed at my own answer. "I don't know."

He's coming. Replayed in my mind.

...

We went back to Lev's shop, hoping he'd have some insight into using my unknown Fae blood.

His large jowls hung down in a frown. "I'd rather not use your blood," he lamented, confirming my earlier hunch, "for a variety of reasons." His drawn-out sigh rumbled his protruding stomach. "However, it appears to be the only option we have."

"What could happen?" Bray asked.

Lev shrugged his yellow-clad shoulders. "Anything, honestly, but hopefully, nothing." He turned from the counter, heading to the door marked OFFICE. "Let's begin."

Lev's office didn't make use of the daylight-mimicking fixtures that the rest of his shop did, and the effect was eerie.

"Why are there no windows?" I questioned, irritated.

"It used to be strip joint," Lev replied.

I opened my mouth to question, but Bray waved it away. "Later."

A long velvet couch of some dark shade rested against the back wall, next to an end table of a lighter shade, and a glass lamp that gave off just enough light to reveal its crystal shade of blue, red, and green, but nothing further. We stopped at a round table, each taking a seat, while Lev brought over a bowl he had prepared earlier.

He set it down in front of me, along with a jewel-encrusted blade. I looked at the glittering gold hilt, and a pit opened in my stomach.

"It's from Fae," he answered to my unspoken question. Hesitantly, I picked up the hilt, not allowing my mind to travel further along this horrid path, before closing my hand around the blade.

Blood trickled onto the golden hilt as I was shoved into a vision.

The stars surrounded me in a space devoid of time.

"Sister!" a voice boomed.

Colors began to swirl together, red, gold, and blue, attempting to take shape, yet unable to solidify.

"Who are you?" I asked, my voice softer, gentler in this realm of vastness.

"What?" he asked, taken back.

"Who are you?" I repeated again, infusing strength into my timber.

"Your brother," he replied, his voice softening, "Kolm."

"Kolm," I repeated the name, finding that something in my soul knew of it. "Kolm."

"You don't remember me?" his voice was wounded, and I sought to assuage it.

"I remember nothing," I whispered, before gaining strength. "I REMEMBER NOTHING!"

I awoke screaming, Bray shaking my shoulder, worry etched into her features. Snapping up from my seat, I pushed her off, exiting Lev's shop as though the evil within the vision was chasing me.

Was Kolm evil? Was Kolm the "he" my internal voice was warning me about?

92

Chapter 9

The note I found on my door in the mid afternoon was from Bray, confirming that they—she and Seth—had successfully lured and killed the Baubas. I crumpled it before heading inside to shower. My time away seeking answers had led to only more questions. Not bothering to rest after my night of feasting on foul beings, I went to Bray's.

Was I ignoring who I thought I was? Absolutely.

I raised my arm to knock, when a thud inside the apartment jerked me to attention, followed by a crashing. I paused for a moment, waiting for Seth or possibly Bray's mother to speak, but nothing met my ears except grunts and hisses.

I wasn't delusional enough, yet, to believe this was normal.

When the handle wouldn't yield under my force, I kicked the door in, happily adding myself to the ongoing fight within. Wasting no time, I punched through one foul ghoul's spine, ripping it out along with his head. No sustenance to be had here, it seemed. Boo.

The next one came quickly. Clawed hand extended, it raked across my cheek before I could duck. I clawed my way through its decrepit rib cage and pulled out its unbeating heart. Still it came at me. My next blow removed the head.

"Bray!" I screamed, "DUCK!" I lobbed the head at the attacker whose teeth were precious inches away from her throat. Bray wouldn't heal like me. That bite would mean death.

She sliced through her next attacker, her gun lying spent and useless on the floor. I put my back to her, flexing my claws as another round came at us.

"Where are these fucking things coming from?" I demanded.

"Portal," Bray panted. I turned, seeing the blood oozing down her side.

"We have to get you out of here," I clipped out.

"We have to close the portal. If they get by us, these monsters will destroy the city." Her words held a truth I knew to my soul, even as I struggled to understand the finer details of it.

"How do we close the portal?" I asked.

She shook her head, energy waning.

"Can you ward yourself?" I asked.

She nodded.

"Do it," I commanded her.

Using the blood from her side, she created the ward, three circles around, three levels of protection. I knew it couldn't save her from one like me. But the first ghoul that attacked it was unable to penetrate.

"Good," I muttered, moving deeper into her apartment to find the source of our problems.

Next to her bed an oval loomed, suspended over the now blood-red carpets, ghouls fighting to escape from it. With a sigh born of something deeper, I held on, my hands on either side of the portal. The decaying monsters latched onto me, teeth digging into my flesh, claws finding purchase in my loose clothing.

Slowly, I pressed my hands together. The thin gold band around the portal wavered under my force and I renewed it, knowing I could do this, knowing this portal wasn't stronger than me. The golden band cracked, and the ghouls trapped halfway out struggled more. Blood trickled down my cheek, my right shoulder burning from where one had attempted to remove my arm.

With a battle cry, I snapped the band, dissipating the portal. The blowback sent me hurtling into the wall. Random pieces of ghoul crawled over the floor, mixed with gold from the portal.

"Andy?" Bray called out, fear tracking her words.

"I'm fine," I groaned. Standing, I began methodically removing heads from torsos. "Your room, however, isn't."

I stumbled into the living room that doubled as her office. Holding my hands up, I sent a blast into the remaining ghouls, turning them into dust.

"That's so much faster, why didn't I start with that?" I muttered, slipping onto the couch.

"Andy, we need to get to medical," Bray's skin looked multiple shades paler than normal.

"Agreed, exit the wards so we may go," I muttered.

Bray nodded, breaching the circles with her blood.

I hefted myself off the couch, catching her under the arm when she staggered.

"Elevator?" I asked.

"Yeah, let's see if it's working," she muttered, slipping into oblivion.

...

Thankfully, one of the elevator buttons was marked with a large M, and I made the assumption that would take us to the lower level where medical attention could be had.

The doors slid open to armed guards and I scowled, "Your presence would have been helpful earlier."

They moved to block me. Towering fools, they held no sway and no power over me.

"BRAY!" Zander screamed, coming around the guards, he slipped under her other arm, helping with her weight. The guards pressed closer, sniffing me and growling.

"Back off!" Zander barked. "Tomolin, get them back," he bellowed.

"At ease, my guards," said a short man with black hair, thick glasses on his nose. "Bring her here." He indicated a sterile bed along the wall, and we hoisted her weight onto it.

"What happened?" Zander asked in horror, looking over the gurney at me.

"Move, both of you," Tomolin demanded.

I slunk back to the wall, sliding down it, not caring that I was leaving a bloody trail.

"She had ghouls in her apartment," I recounted.

"How the fuck did they get in?" Zander barked.

"Portal," I conveyed.

"Impossible," one of the guards dismissed. It took me a few moments to identify them as the shifters that Bray had said guarded this place. Perhaps I was hurt more than I realized.

I shrugged, pain burning through my right shoulder. "You are not required to believe me."

"No one can open portals into this structure, it's warded against that kind of thing," the second guard informed me.

"Wards are only as powerful as those who cast them," I muttered, resting my head back. Healing sleep was coming.

The guard kicked me with a booted leg but I kept my eyes closed. "Careful," I warned, "the ghouls offered me no sustenance, and I could easily drain you to heal my wounds." I cracked an eye open. "Or I can sleep, you decide."

With wide, fearful eyes he backed up. "What the hell did you let in here?" he questioned Zander.

...

I awoke with a cramp in my neck, not easily assuaged as I rolled my head and massaged the offending muscles.

"Sleeping beauty's finally awake," Bray teased. It was easy to hide my relief with my eyes closed and head bowed.

"You survived," I muttered, slowly prying my eyes open and bringing my gaze to hers.

She shrugged, her skin tone still pale, dark circles under her midnight blue gaze. "I'm hard to kill." She looked around the small room and I followed her gaze. "Thank you," she whispered.

I nodded, "Never thank a Fae, Bray, we'll steal your soul without you even knowing it."

She huffed, blinking back tears. "Right," she groaned.

"Relax, I'm into soul energy, and you're running low at the moment." She laughed and I smiled.

"Zander is going to have a lot of questions for you," she warned. "I told him I didn't know how you closed the portal, but you should know, being able to do so makes you Royal Fae."

"Royal?" I muttered, pulling away the ruined clothing from my right shoulder and seeing the angry wound still healing.

"Royal, as in from a Royal family, as in someone has to be missing you," Bray finished.

I looked at her, blinking, my brows furrowed. "I don't remember." I didn't want to.

Her worried gaze softened. "I know."

Yelling from outside drew our attention, and I moved to open the door.

"Please, please don't do this! I didn't know! I didn't know," sobbed a human.

"Will you stay and heal?" I asked Bray.

She stood next to me, scoffing, "Any more dumb questions?"

"Not at the moment," I conceded and followed the sound of distress.

We entered what appeared to be Tomolin's office. "What are you doing out of bed?" the medical man asked, coming to steer Bray into an office chair. She allowed it.

"We heard there was a party and felt neglected we didn't get an invite," Bray muttered, watching Zander pause with a wicked-looking blade held to the man's neck.

"He was in your room. He's part of the maintenance crew. We think he left something there," Zander explained, while Seth held the man down.

"We don't hurt humans," Bray reminded them.

"He's not human," I said around a yawn.

All eyes turned to me.

"What is he?" Tomolin asked cautiously.

"Ghoul, newly made," I informed them.

The man's eyes widened, "No, no she said that's not how it works."

I shrugged, "She lied."

"No, no," he began fighting in earnest now and Seth was struggling to hold him.

"I swear, it's like you've never properly interrogated someone before," I muttered. I sauntered over, then slammed my hands onto either side of the chair, lowering my face even with the newly made monster.

"Now, you'll be staying here and I'll be asking questions. If you decide not to answer, I'm going to split your skull open and find the answers in there myself." I hadn't thought it was possible to see more of the whites around his eyes, but I was wrong.

"You're going to kill me!" he screeched, looking down at the blade protruding from his chest.

"Oh yes, that's a given," I laughed with a shrug. "But you get to decide how much pain you suffer before you leave this world." I leaned in next to his ear. "And I truly hope you pick the harder path."

I pulled back, a fanged smile on my lips, claws extended.

"Let's begin. Who created you?" I asked.

His lips clenched together. I clicked my claws together.

"Someone you care for deeply," I whispered, running a claw over his cheek. Seth and Zander had backed up, both watching me intently.

"A lover?" I questioned, noting the slight widening of the eyes before he continued his scowl.

"Did you bring her here?"

Rapid blinking, trying to remember.

I narrowed my gaze. "What else did she have you do?"

He scoffed, "I'm never telling you."

I grinned, wrenching his head back. "I was hoping you'd say that."

...

Tomolin was the only one who remained throughout my interrogation. Everyone else fled once I cracked the man's skull open, hunting for answers. The healer handed me a clean towel, and I casually wiped brain matter off my fingers.

"Does that technique work with all Supernaturals?" Tomolin asked.

"I don't believe so. Ghouls lack the natural barriers of protection..." I began, although I couldn't finish.

"How did you know he was newly turned?"

"The smell," I said with a shrug.

"Do you find it strange, being able to access the information you need in critical situations, but not your memories?" he asked, pushing his glasses up on his nose.

"I find everything to be strange lately," I confessed.

He nodded. "May I look at your shoulder?"

"No," I barked, turning away. "It's healing, thank you,"

He nodded again as Bray came back into the room. "You were right, he did lay three other portal traps in the building. How did you know?"

"He's a valuable asset. They'd have used him extensively before giving his position away to target you," I answered, not adding, it's what I would have done—distract and attack.

Bray's lips thinned.

"Are we going to talk about this being the third attack on you?" I questioned.

Her gaze flipped up to mine, and the conversation was closed with a short shake of her head.

I nodded. "Any chance there is a bounty on him? I need new clothing."

Bray sighed and shook her head.

"Sad, do let me know when you're up to hunting again. I'm down to one outfit. At this rate, I'll be walking around naked soon," I said with a shrug.

Seth stormed off the elevator, stalking toward Bray. "You're coming home with me," he grunted. She pulled her arm out of his hold.

"I'm not putting the pack in danger because of one attack," she hissed at him.

"Three," I added. Seth's clear blue gaze swung to me in shock before turning back on Bray.

"Three." He held up his fingers as though we were toddlers, hurt clearly lacing his words. "This is the third attack on you," he rasped out.

"Snitch." Bray grunted.

"The attacks are gaining ground," I shrugged. "The next one is sure to be more powerful, probably enough to kill you. I like you, so I'd rather not rush right into attack number four. Even with all your skills and knives and guns, continuing this way alone is going to get you killed."

"And you think going with him is the right option? They have families and kids where he lives," Bray snapped at me.

I blinked, something worming up my brain, squinting my right eye. I tried not to concentrate on the sensation. "We need to change the landscape. Clearly, whoever is targeting you has done their homework. They know where you work and where you sleep, and they've been planning this long enough to infiltrate the maintenance department here. They will have several backup plans. You must choose a location that they will have to scramble to attack."

Seth looked at me wide-eyed. "Who are you?" he asked.

I waved his question away. "What would be your next step, Bray, acting alone?"

She scuffed the floor with her boot. "I'd track down how the portal was made," she confessed.

"How?" I asked.

Tossing her black hair, she met my gaze, "I have a few contacts."

"Do you use them often?" I asked.

She shrugged, "When needed."

I nodded, "I have an idea."

Chapter 10

"This is the worst idea," Zander complained as he put his SUV in park in front of Lev's shop.

The mirroring spell had jumped into my brain unbidden, presenting a perfect solution.

Through the earpiece, I'd be able to hear Bray while wearing her appearance. The magic had taken both Seth and Zander by surprise, and I was certain my newfound status of Royal Fae was now known by all. I couldn't place why exactly that upset me, knowing only that it made me exceptionally wary.

"Lev!" Zander called into the deserted shop. "LEV!" he called out louder when there was no response.

"Aye, aye, shut your pie hole, I'm coming," muttered a voice ambling through the stacks at the far end of the room. "Always yelling, always screaming, Zander, so much anger," Lev muttered.

I tilted my head at Zander, wondering what Lev was picking up on. Certainly, it shouldn't be a surprise that Zander was angry someone had targeted Bray; the two seemed close.

Lev climbed the steps behind the counter, bringing him almost up to our height.

"Ehh—you're not Bray!" he screamed, backpedaling away from my false face before squinting at me. "Andy?" he questioned.

I smiled. "There have been three attacks on her life, but she's safe." I produced part of the gold ring, scavenged from the floor of Bray's bedroom, from my pocket. "We are hoping you can help us track down the ones responsible." The lure proved too strong to ignore, and he quickly came forward for the gold.

"Ones," he muttered, looking over the golden piece without touching it. "Not just one?" he emphasized, peering up at me.

I shook my head. "I will not slant you with my view. Examine and report," I commanded. The familiarity of giving those orders, I ignored.

Zander stepped forward, pulling me back a step. I allowed it—not happily, but I did. "I'd remove your hand," I warned him.

"Why?" he demanded, keeping his hand in place.

I turned to bark at him, "Because I am hungry, and you can either fuck me or fight me to nourish me." I pulled back.

"If you two want to come back, it'll take me sometime to finish," Lev offered with a thin smile.

"No," Zander answered for the both of us, "we'll wait."

...

Waiting ended up meaning sitting against the shop wall, keeping Lev squarely in our sights.

"Let me eat him when we are done," I requested.

"No, we don't eat friends," Zander answered, annoyed.

"Is he really a friend, though?" I questioned. "One of Bray's contacts has betrayed her. It could be him."

"Or it could be the next contact on our list," Zander pointed out. "Or someone with a longstanding grudge, someone who doesn't like half-breeds, someone who is trying to distract from bigger issues, someone from a case who didn't like how she talked to them. The options are limitless."

I sighed, "Your logic is unfortunate."

"Would you really eat him and not feel bad?" he asked.

Lev cleared his throat. "I've finished."

With a groan, we heaved ourselves off the floor.

Thick spectacles sat on Lev's nose, enlarging his wide eyes.

"Report," I demanded with a wave of my hand.

"You have terrible manners," Lev insulted me.

"I will eat your soul," I threatened.

"Is she serious?" Lev demanded.

"Unless I fuck her," Zander shrugged.

"You should do that," Lev hissed.

I chuckled, "Either way, your are infringing on my eating, so let's go." I waved my hand impatiently.

"The ring is solid gold. There are trace essences from several races of the Fae, all minor races, not that powerful separately, and one high Fae trace."

"How were the essences taken?" Zander asked.

"Blood, is my guess," Lev shrugged. "Organs, sexual fluids ... there are other ways, depending on what the caster needed it for."

"Can we track it?" I asked, hoping for a meal.

Lev shook his head. "No, the residuals are too weak. Honestly, I never would have believed this could be done if I hadn't seen it."

"List all the races of Fae present," I demanded.

...

Zander looked over the list. "How would someone obtain blood from this many races?"

"We are Fae," I groaned at him on a sigh. "We're hunting a female, one who—what's the nice way you say it?—oh yeah, sleeps with many different types of Fae. Can you think of an establishment where that kind of thing goes on, and can I find a meal there?"

Zander's eyes widened, before narrowing. "I'm not taking you there."

"Who, then? The real Bray, so she can finally be put down?"

He slammed me against the car and I ground my hips against him. "Careful, I think I like it rough," I whispered before nibbling his ear.

"I'm perfectly capable of protecting her. Get in the fucking car," he ground out, making his way to the driver's side.

We called Bray over the speakers of Zander's car, which I had to admit was a nice one.

"Andy, why isn't your phone charged?" she complained once we had updated her.

"Why does the black box need to charge?" I asked.

"So people can call you?"

"Who would call me? I live in your housing unit now."

Bray sighed. "I was trying to text you."

"What is text?"

"Oh, for—we will have this conversation when you get back. I'm going with you to Sinners Lounge," she clipped out.

"Good, we will be right there," Zander quickly answered.

I sealed my lips on the mistake they were making. It was their lives, they were free to do what they wanted with them. But one way or another, I was going to find myself a snack.

...

"This is how you text," Bray instructed me on the drive to Sinner's Lounge. The screen on my phone, newly charged by Bray, illuminated with words in glowing green bubbles.

"Fascinating," I muttered. I grudgingly followed her directions as we sent a few messages back and forth.

Zander turned around in the front seat. "If you two are done, we've arrived."

"Finally," I grunted, "I am starving."

"Don't kill anyone," Zander snipped in his usual, miserable manner.

"Anyone who doesn't deserve it," Bray amended with a smile. Her dark hair was curled and a black skirt replaced her usual jeans. On top, she sported a flowing tank (my latest lesson in clothing vocabulary), with a deep, v-shaped neck. Zander offered his arm with something almost resembling a smile, and they went to stand in line. Letting a few couples slip in between us, I also stood in the horrendous test of Andy's patience.

I didn't enjoy it, and I texted Bray as much. I pointed out the merits of eating said line to hurry this process along. I was adamantly told no.

Once we made it inside, the throng of people was intense. I found myself hungrily sipping from emotions running rampant. While it wasn't as satisfying as sucking a soul dry, it eased the throbbing in my temples. Perched on a bar stool, overlooking the dance floor, my gaze was drawn to the multitude of species in this establishment.

"Whatcha drinking?" the bartender asked with an easy smile and a missing shirt.

I ordered a drink, hoping for a liquid to delight my taste buds.

"Coming right up." He peeked over at me as I watched him work. "First time in?" he asked.

I nodded, before shrugging, "That I can recall."

His hand stilled over the ice. "Oh yeah?" he questioned.

I nodded again as he delivered the drink to me.

"Lose your memories?" he asked, using the rag slung over his shoulder to wipe his hands.

"After a fashion, I suppose."

"Huh, are you trying to get them back?" he pushed.

I raised an eyebrow at him. "I certainly wouldn't be opposed, and I didn't know it was possible."

He nodded. "Go to the red elevator, top floor. Ask for Axel." I hesitated for a moment. Bray and Zander hadn't requested my protection, nor had they stayed in view so I could provide it. Shrugging, I decided to pursue this lead.

I nodded my thanks, paid my paper money, and wove my way around in search of the red elevator. Nerves beat around my stomach as I questioned if I did indeed want to regain my missing memories. The temptation proved too strong, and I when I arrived at the red elevator, tucked away under a stairwell, I entered it with equal measures of hope and trepidation.

After potentially the longest elevator ride in history, the metal doors opened to reveal a long bar against the right wall, a couch, and floor-to-ceiling windows overlooking the city. I was drawn to the pin pricks of light, even as I sensed another being joining me.

"Beautiful isn't it?" he rumbled.

I shrugged. "The lights are entrancing, but the people, I find them lacking," I confessed.

He chuckled. "What are you doing in my home, pretty girl?"

I turned to him. Thick, midnight stands circled around the crown of his head, and matching onyx eyes peered at me, surrounded by thick lashes.

"Actually, you are pretty," I muttered.

He smiled, revealing dimples. One thick arm came to brace against the window, trapping me. "I'll ask again, why are you here?"

"The bartender downstairs said Axel could help with missing memories," I answered. "But I'm happy to find other things we can do," I said with a smile, wrapping my hands around his jacket.

Perfectly sculpted lips smiled down at me.

"Not picky, are you?" he rumbled.

"Just hungry," I confessed.

He pulled back, eyes dancing with mirth. "I don't have food here."

"I can feed in other ways," I said with a smile.

He let out a groan, lips dipping down to mine. "You are highly tempting," he muttered.

The elevator rang and he groaned, "Hold that thought."

"We got a problem in the main level, Axel. Someone's asking too many questions," a beefy enforcer reported.

"Can you not handle it?" Axel growled. "I'm entertaining." He waved a hand toward me.

"It's probably Bray," I said with a shrug.

"Bray? The Fae hunter? Why is she here?" Axel demanded, quickly returning his attention to me.

"A Fae woman is trying to kill her. One who used life essences from several Fae races in a never-seen-before move to open a portal."

"Portal to where?" Axel questioned.

I shrugged again, turning back to the city lights. "Somewhere they stored an impressive number of ghouls. Such a waste, couldn't even eat their souls."

"Why come here?" the enforcer asked.

"Where else might a female encounter various races of Fae and their reproductive juices?"

"Fuck," they both hissed.

"Get rid of them," Axel snapped at the guard. "But don't hurt them," he added before the elevator doors shut. The guard's gleeful smile fell at the added instruction.

"Friends of yours?" Axel asked, leaning on the arm of the couch, arms crossed, legs braced wide.

I sauntered between his legs. "Define friends," I teased.

"Huh. Okay, this is going to hurt." His hands slammed onto either side of my head, and before I could pry them off, I was falling, down, down, down into darkness.

...

"She's fucking harmless to you!" Bray's voice penetrated the fog of my half-formed thoughts.

"You don't even know what she is," Axel warned.

Zander began with a sigh, "Clearly, some Fae wanted her gone, and she's our problem now."

"She's fucking Fae Royalty!" snapped Axel. "You don't look surprised, Bray."

"I have no idea what you are talking about," she snipped back.

"Royalty is deranged and dangerous, we all know that. There is a reason so many Fae are fleeing Faery right now. You need to put her down," Axel warned, "before whoever put her here comes looking for her."

"She's not bad. She has literally saved my life, three times I might add!" Bray snapped.

"Have you ever asked her why?" Axel questioned.

"Because I'm her only friend, and she hates making friends," Bray reluctantly informed the group.

"Whatever spell or curse she is under is death magic. I touch it and she dies. I uncover it, she dies. I just poke at it, she dies. Someone really, really doesn't want her to remember who and what she was."

"We can just stick her back in Fae," Zander offered.

"She'd be slaughtered," Bray snapped at him, disgust heavily lacing her words.

"She shouldn't be our problem," Zander insisted. "Finding out who is targeting you is. Speaking of which, Axel, are you going to give us the information we need?"

"No," Axel ground out, "I'm going to send you on your fucking way with a problem I neither want nor need."

With the fog now cleared, I pushed up from the floor. "So, this means we're not getting naked and sweaty?"

"Correct," Axel snarled, pounding the elevator open. "Leave."

...

Once we were safely in the car, Bray asked, "How much did you hear?"

"Enough," I replied quietly, staying silent for the remainder of the ride.

Chapter 11

It wasn't until the next morning, waiting for Bray to get ready for our next case in my apartment, that I used my voice again.

"Why are Fae fleeing Faery?" I asked, prepared to be shot down.

Bray sighed, pushing the paperwork away to look me over. "Faery isn't a pleasant place. It's divided into four sections, each with its own King and Queen. The Summer Court, Autumn Court, Winter Court and Spring Court. For thousands of years, they coexisted in something vaguely resembling harmony."

"Until?" I pressed.

She sighed, "Until Fae began dying."

She heaved in a breath and pushed on, "The world itself is magic, and its life force, so to speak, sustains the entire realm, along with the Fae who live there. Within the last few Fae lifetimes, something shifted and no one knows how to fix it. Well, Summer Court thinks they do, by killing off entire races and returning their bodies to Faery. The idea, I've gathered from others, is that having fewer mouths to feed, fewer life forces to sustain, should keep other Fae alive longer. The Summer Court has taken over the Spring Court, and now has its sights set on Autumn."

"What of Winter?"

"The King of Winter Court went mad after his wife and child died, and turned the entire court into a torture chamber. The Summer Court uses his services often. I've heard horrid things about it from those who survived."

"Oh," I answered, having nothing to add or say to that. But the need to know more still swirled in my memory-less head. "Is Faery beautiful?" I asked softly.

Bray shook her head. "I've never been and I never will. Half-breeds are killed once discovered, so there is nothing there for me except misery and betrayal."

I nodded. It sounded like an awful place. So why did my heart constrict at never seeing it again?

"If you are looking for more information on the Fae Courts, talk to Zander. He escaped from there and knows more about the types of Fae as well. He helped organize us to be able to take care of and protect each other."

"I don't think he likes me," I muttered, looking at the case file upside down.

"He doesn't like anyone. Rumor is he had his power stolen by Andromalius, and he's afraid she's going to find him and finish the job." Bray shrugged. "Andromalius is the Princess of the Summer Court. She's as ruthless and as awful as you could imagine."

"I can imagine much," I replied honestly.

Bray tilted her head for a moment, before dismissing the question forming there. "Anyways, I was hoping to crash here for a few nights. The new maintenance crew is still fixing up my room, and the medical floor isn't much fun to sleep in when I'm not in immediate danger of dying."

I nodded. "You'll need something to sleep on."

"I have an air mattress." There was a pounding on the door.

"Bray! I know you're in there!" Seth yelled.

I opened the door with a huff. "Now everyone knows Bray is in here." I tilted my head at him. "Why do you pound?"

"She's coming with me to the den," he grunted, pushing past me and slamming a suitcase at her feet.

"You, me, den. Now," he growled.

Bray looked down at the suitcase, before looking up to meet Seth's narrowed eyes. "Did you go through my things?" she asked softly.

He grunted, in agreement or defiance, I wasn't sure.

"And what?" she spat, crossing her arms over her chest. "I don't agree to this, and you'll toss me over your shoulder like a cave man?"

"Don't forget, I'll also spank that plump ass pink." He bent down, threatening or seducing her. Again, I wasn't quite clear which.

"I will not put those families and babies in harm's way!" she bellowed impressively at him.

"We're going to my cabin, no one can get in there," he hissed at her.

"It's warded?" I asked.

"No, but I'll be there," he boasted, turning his attention to me.

"So, you are warded?" I was genuinely confused.

"No." Seth pinned me with his stare, the untamed beast behind pushing against his human façade.

Bray sighed. "What Andy is trying to say is that if they were able to breach the U, they can get in anywhere."

"Anywhere without wards," I corrected.

"But they got in here," Bray protested.

"Because they breached the wards from the inside. The maintenance department was allowed access to your entire apartment, correct?"

"Yes," Bray replied, uncertain where I was going.

"Wards applied over a disruptor are useless."

"How do you know these things?" Bray wondered. "And how isn't this public knowledge?"

I shrugged. "I wish I knew, and Fae sure aren't forthcoming with their secrets," I responded honestly.

"So you're saying you can protect her?" Seth demanded, slightly confused on the use of wards.

"I've already gone over and eliminated any possible disruptor. My wards are strong." I shrugged, "I haven't seen any others that compare to them."

"So you are staying here, with the unknown Fae, with her supposed crazy strong wards?" he pushed.

"For the moment," Bray agreed.

"I am trying to help you," he hissed.

"I appreciate it, but I don't need it," she explained to his backside as he stormed out.

"What else do you know of wards?" Bray asked.

"I don't know. Ask me the right questions, and we'll find out."

...

My sword dripped the blood of the ingrates. Miserable pieces of Faery waste. How they survived this long was a mystery, one I refused to waste any time on.

Another urchin hiding under a filthy rag, my sword swooping soundlessly, ending the pathetic waste.

"Sister, we ride," said a man with fair hair.

I nodded, surveying the destruction we had leveled here.

"Will we ever be done?" I wondered aloud.

His gaze cut to where our Father tended to the dragons.

"Never, until we cleanse Faery of the evil ruining it," he hissed to me.

I cleaned my blade on the apron of a fallen woman, her eyes wide and glazed over in death.

"Forgive me, brother," I bowed. *"I am simply tired."*

"You should retire early, sister, so that your head doesn't roll with the disbelievers killing our beloved Faery."

I nodded. He was correct, family or not. Faery was dying, a slowly wasting existence due to overpopulation and a lack of reverence for the old ways. A mistake and oversight my brother and Father sought to fix, but it didn't mean...

Mounting up, I looked over the fields. Crops burned, bodies left out carelessly, the land unable to reclaim them due to the level of evil residing in them. How had we strayed so far from our true natures?

...

I woke with a scream trapped in my lungs.

Remember, remember me, whispered a voice. Jumping from the bed, I scanned the darkened room, hoping there was an enemy, that my wards had failed and not my mind.

There was no one with me and I wasn't so delusional as to lie to myself, so after checking that Bray slept soundly with undisturbed wards, I took myself down to medical.

Tomolin looked at me through thick glasses in his office, fear and interest warring .

"Zander," he hissed in warning, and I raised an eyebrow.

Zander turned from whatever laid in front of him. How had I missed him there?

"Andy?" he responded, using my name as a question.

"You sure are here a lot," I muttered, unsure about admitting my weakness in front of him.

Zander shrugged, the usual malice gone. "I live close by. What do you need?"

"I'm hearing voices," I admitted, fear my unpleasant companion.

"What kind of voices?" Zander questioned, nodding to Tomolin, who walked us into an open room before shutting the metal door firmly behind him. Through it all, he kept peering at me from behind his rounded frames, uncertain.

"How often?" Tomolin asked, moving into action.

"A few times," I confessed.

"What did they say?" He shined a light into my eyes, then felt under my neck.

"'Remember, remember me,'" I whispered, tears slipping down my cheeks.

Tomolin touched my cheek, sharing a look with Zander. His finger tip was red. Wiping at my cheek, I found my hands came away the same.

"I need to gather more testing equipment," Tomolin announced, not waiting for a response before he pulled the door closed behind him.

"Is this normal of Fae in this world?" I wheezed out, my voice and nerves failing me.

"No," Zander admitted, "it's not."

"I appreciate your honesty," I whispered, closing my eyes and willing strange and unknown sensations in my chest to ease.

"I dreamed of Faery," I managed through clenched teeth.

The table dipped as Zander added his weight, his thigh pressed against my own. I dared a look at his espresso eyes, expecting a blade, a fight, not the compassion, not the concern. I should push him away, I thought, mock him for such weakness.

Instead, I pulled a ragged breath.

"What did it look like?" he asked.

"Death, and dragons," I whispered.

"What?" He leaned closer, taking my hand. "Did you say—"

I nodded. "An entire village killed, destroyed … cleansed." The last word burst forth in absurdity, leaving me shaking my head.

"Cleansed," he repeated, his voice hardened.

I nodded, meeting his gaze through the red haze in my own. "Even children," I hiccupped.

His steady gaze was his only reply.

"I don't understand these feelings!" I cried out, slamming my fists against my thighs. "I understand nothing," I whispered, the blood tears falling freely now. The woman in my dreams harbored no such sorrow, but here in this moment, with the horrors of the dream chasing me, I felt guilt, rage, and hopelessness.

"It's sorrow, Andy. This is deep, unyielding sorrow."

"I hate it," I gritted, latching onto an emotion that at least made sense.

Zander chuckled, rubbing my back. "I know, kid, I know."

"I'm not a child, I—" I couldn't say it. I couldn't voice it, that I had killed children. I had ended an innocent's life, maybe many of them.

Zander blew out a breath as Tomolin burst back in, using a clear tube to collect my tears before plucking a strand of hair from my head.

"What did Axel say?" Tomolin asked, adding a variety of colored liquids to the sample he had collected.

"That I'm death cursed. Any attempt to bypass or access the spell will kill me," I flatly informed him.

"Huh," Tomolin muttered. "Who are you, that someone would go to such trouble? Perhaps an answer lies in that."

"I'm no one," I whispered. "Certainly someone would know my face if I was of import?"

Tomolin shrugged. "Fae look different in different dimensions. Faery naturally enhances what it has created, but even so, some Fae are dependent on glamour in both realms due to their horrible nature."

"Like the dryad," Zander offered.

"He wasn't horrible," I shrugged, "although his dental hygiene did leave much to be desired."

Zander barked a short bust of laughter.

"Anything?" he asked, turning his attention to Tomolin, who furiously studied the unchanging vials.

"No, which is odd." Tomolin sighed, looking at me over the frames that had slipped down his nose. "It's powerful magic, Andy, I'm sorry. I don't have an answer for you this evening." He pushed his glasses up. "I'll see what research I can do. We have other healers here, along with a few texts we managed to save from the cleansing."

I nodded, whispering, "Thank you."

A knock on the door drew our attention. Zander hopped down from his seat next to me, and the loss of his warmth sent a shiver up my spine.

Liz peeked in, a false smile pulling up her lips. "So sorry to interrupt, but Zander, can I talk to you?"

Zander looked back at me, and I nodded before he moved to leave the room. I couldn't appear weak in front of Liz.

Tomolin patted my knee. "Take your time, Andy, you're welcome to stay as long as needed." I was unable to voice the piercing of my heart at his words.

Bowing my head over, I pushed against the urge to scream, to wail, to cry and give in to the misery. I had to fight, fight … fight what? What was I fighting against? I let one wracking sob out before refusing another. Steel banded my temples, and it throbbed in time with my heart, my body voicing its displeasure at being denied the space to feel.

Emotions were weaknesses. I knew that, yet here they overwhelmed me, threatening to drown me in unknown memories and potentially ghastly pasts I couldn't even fathom. Was I that monster? Had I taken those lives?

I needed answers. After cleaning my face, I walked back to Tomolin's office, prepared to spend the next week reading texts if it could lead me to my memories. And I had a feeling reading wasn't one of my favorite pastimes.

"I needed you on the drop tonight." Liz's voice seethed with anger and unsaid words.

Zander huffed, "You don't need me for much, sister." Liz growled and I snuck closer to the open door.

"You let an unknown Fae into our inner circle, Liz. Andy is dreaming of dragons, fucking *dragons*." His voice rose and I flinched, backing away from the raw displeasure in it.

A chair scraped. "Only one caste of Fae uses dragons, Liz."

"I'm aware," came her pointed reply.

"What have you brought here?" Zander's question was weary, desperate.

"What I needed to. Stay close to her, she'll be an asset before long." Her confidence in me was misplaced, that much I could have told her.

"Asset?! She's hearing fucking voices," Zander scoffed. His dismissal hurt deeply, more than I would admit.

"What are they saying?" Liz asked, devoid of emotions.

"'Remember, remember me,'" I revealed, pushing the door open and standing in the doorway, feeling small, so small. I wanted to meet Zander's gaze, hoping to find remorse there for his earlier words. But I couldn't do it.

"How am I to be an asset?" I demanded.

Liz shrugged. "I mean, just look at you. Warding skills better than the damn U, fighting skills keeping our enforcers alive, not to mention your soul-sucking skills." Her eyes raked over me at that comment. "Out prowling, are you?"

"I don't know what prowling is," I admitted, quickly losing ground.

"That outfit," she explained, pointing at my tank top and sleep shorts. "Bound to land you some dinner," she chuckled, shooting Zander a glare before leaving.

Looking down at myself, I protested, "Bay said it was sleepwear."

"It's not meant to be worn outside," Zander explained.

I didn't look at him, instead just nodding and heading back to the elevator.

I was pounding on the arrow to bring the metal machine to my rescue when I heard his deep sigh and the scrape of his chair. To my relief, the doors opened and I bounded inside, slamming my palm against the tenth floor and "Close" buttons, as I had seen Bray do when she was in a rush.

Zander's dark head popped out of Tomolin's office. "Andy—" he began, but the rest was lost to the smooth sliding of metal doors, the wards of this wretched world.

I sagged against the back wall. Coming down here had been a mistake of epic proportions.

...

I found myself hiding on the roof, kept company by whirling machines and piping, unable to lie to myself about what I was doing. I had demanded answers, but now that the truth was brewing inside of me, I was doing everything I could to avoid it.

The worst was wondering if I was a threat to Bray. She was the only person in my life who had been honest with me, and now trusted me to keep her safe in my apartment. Could I be a danger to her?

You are a threat to everyone, whispered the voice.

Great. That's so fucking helpful.

Chapter 12

"You made coffee?" Bray grunted to me, shuffling from her room.

"I don't claim to have done it correctly," I offered, staring down into the dark brew cradled between my hands.

Bray filled the only other mug I owned, sitting down heavily next to me at the kitchen bar.

"Did you sleep well?" I asked.

"Like the dead. Guess I killed myself." She chuckled at her own joke, then noting my lack of agreeable humor, squinted one blue eyeball at me. "You?"

"No," I confessed. "Bray," I began, turning to her. "If I—" Gods, how did I explain this? "What if I am evil?"

Bray raised an eyebrow. "Yeah, 'cause evil people totally save helpless kids and then worry about what happens to them."

I huffed. "But what if I was evil before? What if I have done terrible things?" I whispered.

Bray scratched her disheveled ebony hair. "Well, this is a serious conversation happening too fucking early." She drew in a breath and met my gaze, sleep now gone from her. "Look, Andy, if you were evil, you're making up for it now." Her gaze was as genuine as it was unyielding. "You've saved my life and those kids. And you've only been here a few weeks."

She shook her head, taking a sip. "I don't know your past, but I can tell you it doesn't define you here, in this moment. Only your actions do."

I nodded. "Will you put me down if I turn evil?"

She smiled, all teeth. "Absolutely."

"Thank you," I whispered, turning back to my coffee, which was actually tolerable.

"Andy, you are the only one who has ever thanked me for a veiled death threat. And this one wasn't really even veiled."

I shrugged.

"I think you're my best friend," she said around a yawn, which ended in a groan as pounding hit our door.

I went to answer it, moving aside when Seth's glowing frame appeared, a welcome sight compared to the thickly corded and slightly shorter frame of Zander, which I was desperately hoping to avoid.

"You've got a delivery," he hissed, dropping a package in front of Bray before looking over at me. "And you're not the only Supernatural with exceptional hearing. If she doesn't put you down, I will," he smiled, revealing his impressive canines.

Bray gasped before running from the room, the sound of retching trailing behind her.

Seth cleared the few steps to the package quickly, swearing before going after her.

I approached the box with a healthy dose of uncertainty, peeking in to see the head of Lev, mouth opened, thick neck still attached, eyes squeezed closed in terror.

I sniffed the bald head, drawing in stale blood, smoke, and hickory. That didn't offer me much.

"Andy," Bray warned.

I pulled my tongue back into my head. "Yes?"

"Are you really about to lick a dead head?" she asked, slightly intrigued, slightly horrified.

"Yes," I nodded.

"Why?" Seth asked from behind her, hand resting supportively on her shoulder.

"I think I can track the killer that way?" I offered with a shrug.

"Huh." Seth looked down at Bray, who nodded to me.

"Go ahead," she advised, but her defeated look sent a chill of rage through me.

I licked, my eyes rolling back as I relived Lev's last moments.

"Darkness," I whispered. "Wood under his feet…"

Seeing through Lev's eyes, I panted, picking myself up again, the body of water roaring close by, drowning out the sounds of my cry for help and the footsteps of the attacker. I lunged for a blue door, only to be pulled back and ended in a moment.

I drew a long breath, then summarized the scene for Bray and Seth.

"Do it again," whispered Seth, watching me in awe.

"Fairly certain that was a one-time deal," I shrugged. "You wanna try?" I asked, offering him the box.

"No," he pulled back, holding a hand out. "I prefer my animal kills."

I nodded. "I can respect that."

Bray had her arms crossed over her chest, her gaze riveted to the box.

"Take it to Zander," she commanded Seth. "That'll give us a head start. Ugh, no pun intended."

"Head start for what?" Seth demanded, the previous aura of caring and concern gone.

"Hunting down whoever is hunting me. I'm tired of this game." She went into her bedroom without another word.

Seth sat down hard, shaking his head.

"She doesn't want your protection, Seth. She wants your acceptance."

His green eyes darted to mine. "What? Did she say that?"

"No, and you shouldn't take any advice from me. I hear voices," I shrugged.

Seth huffed, closing the lid on the dead head.

"Thanks, Andy," he muttered as I closed the door after him.

"I need to clean the counter," Bray yelled from her room.

"Yep, my thoughts exactly," I informed her as I nipped a finger and drew a purifying ward on the surface.

She stopped, boots in hand, and watched me whispering over the symbol before it burned into nothing.

I nodded at my handiwork. "I meant like a cleansing wipe," she explained.

I shrugged. "I don't own those, and besides, if there was a tracker or some spell attached to the box or head designed to transfer, that sign would destroy it."

"How do you know these things?" she huffed, not looking for answer.

...

Zander had called Bray many, many times.

She hit Ignore on the call again, before shoving the phone into her back pocket. "Be glad he doesn't have your phone number," she grunted.

126

"I don't have my phone number," I pointed out, strolling through another wooden alleyway within walking distance of Lev's shop. To our left, waves rolled in, the ocean triggering various sensations in me, starting with confusion at why I had never noticed the ocean in this miserable world.

"Why does he insist on calling you?" I asked.

She looked over at the waves, drawing in a salty breath. "Because he knows I'm going to track down my own leads on this and not loop him in." She shrugged, her smile fading. "Why is someone trying to kill me?" she asked the sea. I turned another corner, having no answer for that. The options seemed limitless. She did, or rather we did, kill Fae for money. I doubted most were happy about that fact.

...

It took another thirty minutes before Zander arrived at the shop. He was there to go through Lev's records, according to Seth's text message to Bray. There was another message that she wouldn't read or allow me to read, but it turned her cheeks scarlet.

"You don't think anything of value will be there?" I asked her, staring down yet another alleyway.

Bray shook her head. "Lev was headed to the blue door, that's where our answers will be."

I nodded before coming to a dead stop.

She strode next to me, legs braced wide, dark locks plastered against her face by the wind, hands buried in her jacket pockets. "That's it?" she questioned, backing up a step and giving the door its proper berth.

I nodded, running my hands over the wards in the matching blue door frame. "It's powerful, only allowing Fae in." I turned to her. "I don't think you should try to enter."

She scoffed, "Right, half-blood, can't fucking do anything." She kicked a can that bounced against the far wall, scaring the stray cats.

With a snap of my fingers, I killed the wards. "Okay then, after you," I said, holding out a hand.

She looked at me, cobalt gaze narrowing, no doubt trying to decide if I was attempting to kill her.

"Andy, what if that was supposed to keep something *in*?"

Not the direction my mind had taken, I had to admit. I shrugged. "Guess we'll find out," I smiled, pushing open the worn door, tired of waiting for her.

Darkness assaulted us, a sharp contrast from the light of the day we had just vacated.

"Shit," Bray hissed, searching her pockets.

"Silence," I warned, deadly soft.

She stilled, or at least quieted her movements. We were being watched; I could feel eyes upon us, and a collective hush of held breaths.

Bray clicked on her phone flashlight and I scowled. "I'm not saving you today," I growled low.

"Yeah you will, I'm your only friend, remember?" My eyesight had adjusted to discern her cocky grin.

Her flashlight illuminated the handrail, worn and rusting, leading to stairs.

"After you," I muttered, wondering if I could snatch her fast enough if the metal broke under her weight.

She grunted a reply, stepping down cautiously. We slowly made our way down, passing a few windows, all boarded up.

"There's something here," she hissed. I sent my gaze over the barren floor, wondering where the sensation of being watched was coming from.

"There are several somethings," I muttered, annoyed that I wasn't able to pinpoint exactly what those somethings were.

Bray's scraping sounded loud to my ears. "What are you doing?" I hissed.

My eyes followed the scraping to a crack in the floor. "You're on top of it," I muttered, waiting for her to step aside before I lifted the trap door over. The metal stairs continued down, down, into perfect darkness. Along with a host of wards that I cleared for her.

Bray gave me a look before heading down. Her light did little to penetrate that blackness and give us an idea of what we were walking into. But the scurrying sounds didn't bode well.

Eventually, our feet stepped off the metal and onto the soft dirt, compacted and smooth.

"What the fuck is this?" Bray whispered, holding her light up. Rows and rows of poorly constructed tents met our gaze, all the same brown in color. We began inching forward down a row. As we moved, Bray's light would shine on an entranced gaze, only to have it skitter away. Patches of fur met our search as we came into the center of the haphazard town.

Bray stepped onto the wooden circle marking that center.

"We aren't here to hurt anyone," she called out loudly. "A friend of mine was killed outside your door." Hushed scuffling had us turning our attention to the direction it apparently came from, before Bray continued, "I want justice for him."

There were no other sounds. "Please," she called out, "please help me." I didn't fail to notice how her shoulders sagged, nor the tear that slipped down her cheek.

I heaved a sigh. "I won't replace the wards on either of your doors if you don't cooperate." I gave Bray a wicked smile.

A furry, thick animal burst forward on all fours, before rising to his hind feet. "Please, you must replace them! We are hunted here! Hunted by monsters!"

"Define monster?" I asked.

He looked around, watching for others before he stepped closer. "The Shadows are here," he whispered, before scampering back to safety.

"Shadows?" Bray asked, looking to me for clarification.

My gaze narrowed as my mind produced a vision just out of my grasp; tall black trees, perfectly round moons overhead, and the scent of blood everywhere.

I shook my head to dispel it, not willing to look any closer at it, before turning to Bray and shrugging.

I shifted the topic. "Why was Lev trying to come here?"

"We don't know." A woman in the same rounded, furry shape came out, holding a small child on her hip.

"That's not entirely accurate, is it?" I demanded.

She huffed. "What kind of Fae are you, anyway?" she demanded.

"The kind who requires souls for nourishment," I smiled, revealing all my pointy teeth.

She stepped back, holding baby close with a gasp.

"Let's try this again. If you lie to us, I eat your soul. Why was Lev trying to come here?"

"Protection," the woman whispered. "The wards would give him protection against any Fae who wished us ill."

"How did you break them?" the male rasped.

"She snapped her fingers," Bray answered, a smile of pride tugging her lips.

The male looked at me with wide eyes framed in fur. I shrugged. "How did you know Lev?" I asked.

"He's one—he was one of us," the male began again. "You're certain he's dead?" he asked Bray.

Bray swallowed and nodded. "Someone sent me his head in a box," she whispered, another tear tracking. "I asked his help, and it cost him his life. I'm going to bring the fucker who killed him to justice."

"Language," the woman with the baby chided.

...

Hilda, as we now knew the small, furry woman was called, brought us food around a wooden table. "It's not much," she apologized again.

I bit into the bread on a groan. "That's delicious," I complimented her.

Her daughter, Yela, pulled on my jeans, using her slobbery hands to pull herself up unsteadily.

Bray took a bite of the bread and agreed immediately.

"What race of Fae are you?" Bray asked. "I've never heard of or see anyone like you before."

Hilda set down a tray of cheese, fruit, and meat for our greedy stomachs.

"We are the Chitteran, and we've been hiding in the shadows forever." She ended on a long sigh, fingers fumbling with the cloth table covering.

Her husband, Fern, came in and scooped up Yela. "We are seen as a worthless race," he said, cutting right through the bullshit as he sat next to Hilda, who gave him a small nod and sad smile.

"The Summer Court banished us when their King became sick after eating our food. We tried to explain to him that he had been poisoned, but he wouldn't listen."

Hilda sighed, picking up the story. "Banishment wasn't awful at first. Our kind lives to cook for others and while it was sad, we were able to provide and sell what we made, and get what we needed in return."

Fern shook his head. "Until the King got word." I could see the fires in his black gaze, hear the screams of the dying, worthless village.

"They killed everyone they found," Fern continued. "I was just a child and my mother hid me." Resolve straightened his spine as he pressed on, "I have spent my life leading my people out of the hell that is Faery and into an existence that doesn't deem us less than others, simply because of how we look and what our gifts are."

I nodded slowly.

"That still doesn't explain Lev," Bray broached cautiously.

Hilda handed Yela a strawberry. "Lev was the first of our kind to undergo massive surgery so that he looked human," Hilda explained with a shrug.

"We can use glamour," Fern explained, "but it doesn't last long and requires far more energy than we have. Utilizing the human methods had given us some hope."

"So you're hunted because of one mad King?" I clarified.

Hilda shook her head. "Not only that, soul eater." She extended her hand and my brow furrowed.

Closing my eyes, I pulled a slight bit of her soul. Pure light erupted inside of me, and I jumped back, dropping her hand and toppling over the chair.

"You are the untainted," I whispered.

Hilda nodded, sadly. "Our souls fuel the shadows in this world, and so many others."

"Andy?" Bray asked me quietly.

I turned my gaze to her, true worry eating at me. "We have to replace the wards, *now*," I snapped.

Bray nodded. "Thank you for the food, I wish y'all had a delivery service."

Hilda laughed, handing her a paper menu. "We do, although it's all underground at the moment."

Bray nodded her thanks, hesitating, but I was already running toward the stairs and the thin metal piece that didn't seem enough to protect them. I couldn't be trusted around them, I knew that for certain.

"What's untainted?" Bray asked softly after catching up to me.

I sighed, satisfied that my wards would hold. We moved the trap door back into place.

"A legend in Faery says that when we were created, the Gods used only dark magic on some, and only light on others, hoping that we would entertain them with our fighting. However, the Gods who used light were inherently weaker than the dark beings."

"What happened?"

I shook my head. "I don't remember, except that some of the darklings agreed to protect the light. They created a system so that the darklings could feed without killing the beings born of light. But it didn't last. Eventually, the true darkness came and consumed them all."

Bray nodded as we exited and I warded the blue door. "So, the Chitterans?"

"They are one of the few races of true light," I whispered. I watched my magic slithering, wrapping, and intertwining, until I could find no more space to add to it.

"Are these wards as good as what was here?" she asked.

"Better, I warded them against myself as well."

Bray paused in her step. "Why?".

"Bray," I said, placing my hands on her shoulders, "that is an entire race for me to consume. The energy from their souls would give me almost unlimited power. I cannot be trusted not to try to enter again."

Bray nodded. "Okay, got it. So what happens if you do?"

"If I did it correctly, and I did, the curse I carry will be removed."

"Axel said that would kill you," Bray whispered as we approached Lev's shop.

"I'm aware."

...

Zander was waiting for us. "Where have you two been?" he bellowed.

"We had a lead of our own to track down," Bray stated.

"And?" he snipped, brown hair disheveled, glasses askew.

Bray sighed, "We have reason to believe Lev wasn't the race he was claiming."

Zander leaned forward. "Oh really, and what race was claiming?" The vein in his temple throbbed in time with a heart beating loud enough for me to hear.

"He claimed he was descended from the seers," Bray clipped back, not backing down.

"And what do *you* think he was?" Zander bellowed again, slamming a stack of files down onto the concrete.

I sighed, walking around them to enter the shop. Let them bicker.

Paying little attention to the main shop I had seen before, I made my way to the back. Vials upon vials lined each hallway, in carefully constructed shelves on the walls.

"You ever seen something like this before?" Seth asked me, arms crossed over his chest.

"Not that I can recall, for whatever that's worth," I answered honestly.

"What was he into?" Seth demanded.

I sighed. "He claimed to be psychic, but who knows?" I answered, still rather unsure what a psychic was.

"Well, you're going to want to look at this," he shifted the conversation, leading me to a long counter with papers tossed about.

I picked up a picture of me leaving the hospital with Liz, another of me with Bray as we exited our U-shaped building, and finally one of Bray and Seth locked into an intimate moment in the street.

"This explains much," I muttered.

Seth snatched the last photo from me. "He was spying on us."

I shrugged, "Valid." I sifted through more photos. "But was he spying on only us?" I asked.

"That's all we've found, why?"

"We aren't that interesting," I muttered.

"What if he was targeting Bray, and someone did us a favor by taking care of the sick fuck?" Seth spun his theory.

I shrugged, "It's possible, but why the photo of me at my earliest memory?"

Seth sighed, raking his hands through his hair. "You were planted?"

"Also a possibility," I conceded.

Seth sighed, dropping his considerable weight onto a stool. "It doesn't feel right," he finally admitted, letting go of his anger, while still fighting to hide his worry and fear.

"I agree," I answered to all the emotions he was broadcasting.

...

Bray stormed in, Zander right behind her. "I'm not sharing my intel if you won't share yours," he hissed at her.

"Andy, you ready?" she clipped.

"Yep, goodbye Seth." I slipped from my seat, following her out.

...

In her car, Bray slammed the steering wheel an impressive number of times before screaming her frustration.

"Do you want me to drive?" I asked.

She huffed, resting her head on the wheel she had just beaten. "What the fuck is going on here?" she groaned.

"That has yet to be discovered."

"How many more people will die because of me?" Her broken whisper carried easily to me.

"That's a very grand assumption." I raised an eyebrow at her hunched form.

"What?"

"Lev was part of a race thought to be extinct, hunted by the Summer King, who from what you have told me is awful, and he was hiding an entire race a few blocks from his shop."

"His head was delivered to me," Bray snapped.

"Why?"

She blinked at me, "Because I asked him for help."

"That was days ago. If he was being watched closely, wouldn't that have happened immediately?"

"What are you getting at?" Bray asked.

"I think Lev was killed by a shadow walker; I think his head being delivered is something else entirely."

"Why didn't he shrivel up like when you eat souls?"

I shrugged, "I don't know. Where is the rest of his body at?"

"They didn't find it." Bray started the car, driving away.

"Do you think Zander knows of the Chitterans?"

"No, I don't," Bray answered.

I huffed. "Fae are annoying, complicated creatures," I grunted.

She laughed, looking over at me. "Truth."

Chapter 13

The sun was rising, casting Faery in a multitude of soft pinks, along with tangerine orange and a hint of blue sky behind the billowing clouds of smoke choking us all.

Tears fell annoyingly from the cinders of three furry heads, bound together in my hand.

I dropped them at the feet of the war horse before going down on one knee.

"They've been eliminated," I reported.

"All of them?" rasped a voice that grated over my ears.

"All of them," I confirmed.

"Hmm, we shall see," he rasped, before kicking the war horse into a trot.

The view slanted, and I was staring out at Faery from a balcony, with billowing tendrils of fabric around me.

"It's set," a soft-spoken blonde whispered, peeking up at me.

"There can be no mistakes," I hissed.

"No, no lady."

I turned, staring into her green eyes, eerily similar to my own. "He will kill you," I warned her again.

"It doesn't matter, this begins it. You heard the seeing, just as I did. This is the beginning of the end."

That didn't mean I liked it, and my stomach twisted at what she was going to do. I nodded, unable to hold her gaze any longer, the sorrow clenching down onto my throat, squeezing my eyes closed as unwanted tears slipped down my face.

I screamed, a bellow born of rage, of injustice and frustration.

....

"Andy!" Bray screamed, turning on the bedroom light, her gun raised as she searched for the threat.

I screamed again.

Seeing no threat, Bray stowed the gun in her pajama pants. Seth busted in after her, claws extended, as shivers began raking my body.

"Andy," Bray approached me cautiously.

"I lost her," I whispered, fresh tears tracking down my face. I lifted my gaze to Bray, screaming again, "And I don't even know who the fuck she is!"

The sob broke forth and I bellowed once more.

"Bray, back up, she's not stable," hissed Seth.

"Fuck you, Seth, leave if you can't handle it," she reprimanded him, holding out her hands as she crouched in front of me. With hands resting on my shoulders, she reassured, "Andy, it's okay. It's your memories, they're returning. That's a good thing."

"I don't think it is," I whispered. "I don't think I'm going to like who I was."

Bray said nothing, dismissing Seth with a wave as she sat next to me, wrapping her arms around me.

...

Dawn found Bray and me pouring over the files from Lev's office, while Seth, parked on her air mattress, snored loudly.

"How do you not suffocate him in his sleep?" I muttered.

She chuckled, "I'm usually too worn out to hear him." She waggled her eyebrows at me.

"You made a joke!" I laughed.

With an eye roll, she nodded. "Let's check out this supplier. Lev had a delivery ten minutes before he was chased out and killed."

I nodded, "What do they supply?"

"Office supplies, oils, charm bracelets..." Bray took a sip of her coffee.

"That's a wide variety," I muttered.

I tapped a finger against the page. "Do you still have the head?" I asked.

"It's in the morgue." She asked wearily, "Are you going to lick it again?" Her face screamed disgust.

"No, but I'm wondering if we can use the head to locate the rest of the body," I mused out loud.

"You thought the two weren't related, didn't you?"

"I know, but wouldn't knowing who had his body be helpful?" I offered.

She nodded, rubbing the back of her neck. "Supply house first, head licking second."

I rolled my eyes at her.

...

The highly made-up woman at the office supply depot was helpful, providing the last six months' worth of orders by Lev, and the name of the delivery man. He was also cooperative, but didn't have much to offer.

Bray passed me the list in the car with a sigh. "That got us nowhere," she groaned.

I looked over the list. "He ordered a lot," I muttered. "I guess business was doing exceptionally well."

140

Bray shrugged before turning over the engine.

"Dead body?" she guessed.

"Dead head," I clarified.

She groaned.

...

Tomolin wasn't excited to see us.

"Explain to me again how this works?"

"It's a simple tracking spell, to find the rest of him," I told him yet once more, growing annoyed.

"Yes, but he's dead, that tracking spell won't work."

I narrowed my gaze. "Unless we find a necromancer," I said with a smile.

"How do you know these things?" Bray wondered.

I shrugged, "Cursed."

"I think I have a file on a necro we can hunt down," Bray offered. "Animated a college coed for some fun." She scrunched her face up at the thought.

"Interesting," I muttered.

"Gross," she corrected, "the word you are looking for is gross."

I shrugged, "Who I am to judge the sexual tendencies of Fae?"

"Ewwww." She pressed the elevator buttons. "I don't ever want to know what you're into."

"A girl has to eat," I chuckled, enjoying my own joke.

...

Seth was waiting for us in the apartment with a couch, TV stand, and coffee table.

"Where did all this come from?" I wondered, poking the TV he was watching.

"A friend is moving in with his girlfriend and getting rid of stuff. I told him how boring your place was, and he offered me these items for helping him move," he answered, distracted by the television.

"So, you moving in or something?" Bray asked, kicking his feet.

"Or something," he muttered, taking a bite of the pizza he had ordered. "By the way, Andy, my packmate Griffin wanted me to ask if you need to feed, because he is available."

"Yes," I answered with a ravenous smile.

"Keep it in your pants, we have a case." Bray leveled a stare at Seth, before moving to the kitchen table and thumbing through her files.

I was getting a distinct feeling that she wasn't going back to her own apartment.

"Here," she muttered, handing me the file. I squinted at the text as it came into view.

"You need glasses?" Seth asked.

"I don't believe so," I muttered.

"He's in the human jail?" I asked Bray. "How do we get him out?"

"Secretly," she smiled.

I had a feeling I was going to like this.

...

"I take it back, I don't like this," I groaned at her in the back of a police car.

She laughed, "Relax, it'll be over before you know it."

"Let's trade places," I complained.

"Can't, we've arrived." She rolled her window down, handing her fake identification to the real police officer who was guarding the prison gate.

The human prison system was a formidable torture technique, I had to admit.

"I am impressed at the ingenuity of this place," I muttered to Bray. We had changed into medic outfits, taking the very alive body of the necromancer out in the body bag on the gurney between us.

Bray huffed, "I think this is the first thing you've appreciated about Earth."

I shrugged with a small smile. "The potential for torture is ripe, too bad we are in a hurry," I lamented.

Bray shook her head, flashing the needed badges to get us into the white van we used to leave.

...

Antonio the necromancer hung from the handcuffs Bray had strapped him into once we got away from the jail. A dark-haired, thin, and sunken-eyed boy, he didn't appear to enjoy it.

"Do you have to extract Supernaturals from the human law enforcement system often?" I asked.

"Yes. There are the official channels, but they always take too long. This way is faster, and means less humans mucking around in our business," she finished, pinning the Fae with a deadpan stare.

I turned around, drumming my fingers against my chin. "I need to track a dead body," I began.

Antonio scoffed, "I can't do that."

"False, you can," I corrected. "You just need the right spell, and a boost of my power." I smiled, showing all my teeth to his worried face.

"Who the fuck are you?" he demanded, shifting in his chains.

"Just a Fae who's rather hungry, although I don't think I'd eat you," I shrugged.

Bray looked at me, shocked. "What? Who knew you had standards?"

...

"You want me to do what?!" Antonio demanded.

I rolled my eyes in the medical ward while Tomolin looked on, slightly horrified.

"Eat the eyeball," I told him again.

Antonio looked at Lev's dead eyes, covered in white.

"I'd like to go back to prison," he muttered, holding his hands out, I assume for the handcuffs.

I sighed. "No. I need to find the rest of this body, and you are going to do as I say."

Antonio shook his head. "You haven't even explained how this works. I eat the eye and … what?"

"You'll display the resting place out of your own eyes," I informed him.

"You're fucking insane, NO!" He tried to move away from me.

I snatched the back of his head. "One way or another, you are going to consume it," I attempted to negotiate.

Based on his screaming and bucking to getting away from me, it was a failed attempt.

I slammed his head down next to Lev's, before reaching my fingers into the dead man's head for the needed organ.

Antonio flailed around, kicking and screaming, begging someone to help him.

"Andy," Bray said softly, as I shoved the eye into Antonio's screaming mouth and held it shut.

"Yes?" I asked, tightening my grip on Antonio's mouth when he tried to spit it out.

"This isn't right," she began cautiously.

I tilted my head at her. "What isn't?" I asked.

She jutted her chin at Antonio, dry heaving into my hand. Genuinely confused, I asked, "He committed a crime, and yet you have compassion for him?"

"He's not a monster, he just made a bad choice," she replied, covering her mouth at the smell when I released Antonio.

"You feel he deserves a choice? If he didn't comply, we'd have no leads on who is attempting to kill you. I don't regret forcing him to consume the eye. His biology is adapted to consume the dead. If he did that instead of fucking corpses, he'd be stronger than even I."

"You. Are. Fucking. Insane," he hissed, before his eyes rolled over.

"Shit," Bray hissed, pulling out her phone to record it. Darkness, trees, rocks.

"Do you recognize anything?" I asked. Bray shook her head.

The vision snapped off. "I'm going to be sick," Antonio whispered.

I looked down at him retching. "Pathetic," I grunted in earnest disgust.

Chapter 14

Bray played the video again for Seth, since he spent more time in the woods than her.

"Yeah," he admitted with a twitch in his jaw, "I know it." He leaned back against the newly acquired couch in my apartment.

"Great, let's go!" Bray exclaimed, standing and evidently forgetting my earlier moral transgressions.

I ate another bite of chocolate chip cookie dough ice cream, straight from the container, anticipation forcing a gleeful smile across my lips.

"No," Zander stated. "I'll take Andy, but not you."

Bray's previous joy died a horrific death on her now supremely irate face. "What the fuck?" she demanded.

Seth stood as well, avoiding eye contact with her. "You'll get us killed."

I watched the tears prick at her eyes. "Because I'm part human?" she hissed at him.

"Yes," Seth didn't bother to sugarcoat it, though he did finally meet her tear-soaked gaze.

"I. Am. Not. Weak," she hissed at him.

"I know, dammit! But what hunts in these parts," Seth grumbled with a nod to her phone, "would end you before I could even help you! I'm not sure I can get out of there alive myself," he admitted. "But she can," he said plainly, with a point toward me.

I tilted my head at both of them, digging for more ice cream in slow motion and keeping their combined gazes.

"Can I eat what's there?" I asked, licking the back of the silver spoon.

Bray huffed, wiping her eyes. "Fine, but I'm driving you psychos out there."

"Only if Andy wards the car." He looked to me for confirmation, and I nodded.

"Stop being cryptic, Seth," Bray warned.

Seth blew out a breath, leaning forward on the couch, meeting her gaze. "It's a wild gate. The Fae didn't create it, and the humans sure as shit didn't. As far as the packs can tell, who are the only ones aware of it, it's a tear in whatever the fuck separates our world from Faery." He turned to meet my gaze. "And it's a nasty piece of work."

...

"What is this substance again?" I asked, taking another bite of the thick and salty cracker in the backseat of Bray's car. It was a good choice of vehicle to bring if the situation was as dire as Seth's paranoia indicated.

"Pig skins," Seth answered from the front seat, his long legs surprisingly kicked up on the dash.

"I find I enjoy them. Do they take the flesh while the pig still breathes?" I wondered, loudly chomping into another one.

"No, Andy, that's just cruel," Bray corrected me with an irritated sigh.

I shrugged. "Maybe the pig deserved it."

Another hour of driving, and we had arrived. I slammed my hand on Bray's arm. "You are not leave the car," I warned.

"What if I have to pee?" Bray asked, shoving my hand off.

"Urinate in your seat." My gaze flicked over the darkened hills, pulsing with amethyst between midnight trees. The energy throbbed against my temples, in a seductive call I knew to my core. "This is a gate to Faery," I confirmed to Seth.

He nodded.

"Stay with her, Seth. My death would null my wards." Seth nodded, his eyes wide, properly terrified.

I exited the vehicle, biting down hard on my wrist, letting the blood pool. The wards had to go up quickly, in triplicate. The smell of blood would bring out the things of nightmares. Glee bubbled up within me, whether at the thought of those things or returning to the place of my possible home, I wasn't certain and didn't care.

"I will break the wards upon my return." With that, I moved into what I now knew for certain was my home. The transition was gradual, tree trunks blending brown into the inky night, before gaping mouths appeared, along with bones hanging at various angles, revealing a well-fed monster. I wondered who was foolish enough to tempt these beasts. The tingling began in my fingertips, energy and power fluidly washing over me until my entire body vibrated deliciously.

My hands grasped for ... something ... a weapon, I guessed. With a shake, I shifted my claws out, feeling they weren't enough for what lurked here. The path dived down into a valley bathed in purple hues, bleeding into navy and royal blue. A tightness in my chest eased in delight at the sight of magenta flowers with fangs descended, the grass thick and lush under my shoed feet.

I inhaled deeply, scenting the differences between the human realm and Faery, the sense of rightness overpowering.

We could stay here. Be the Queen of the Monsters!

I chuckled. True, but I didn't want to be Queen of anyone, and Bray still needed our help.

We could be the most fearsome monster here, the voice laughed, clearly enticed by the idea.

The sky bled midnight, stars moving to the naked eye. I soaked up the scent of decay, and the floral aroma of irises. It might have been the darkest pit of Faery, but my body had missed it, all the same.

A shuffling had me turning to the left, as a ghoul with a missing jaw ambled toward me from the decaying tree line. "Dammit, I was hoping for a fucking meal," I grunted, before dispatching the rotting annoyance with ease. The ground under my feet rumbled, thick strands of grass rolling like a wave. I stepped back, attempting to get off this ocean of green, only to be pitched forward, landing hard on my hands and knees.

Hands pierced the grass, sending chunks of dirt through the air. Decaying fingers grabbed blindly for me, while their rotting corpses pushed up through the plush turf. More ghouls, ancient and barely strung together with putrid muscles, sprouted out of the tumultuous ground. Staying in the fray was foolish, so I pushed to my feet to get back to the forest and thin out this horde.

Before I'd completed a step, a gaping mouth latched onto my calf. I bellowed at the unexpected pain, slamming my elbow against his skull and watching it explode. Fighting at higher ground wasn't an option, it seemed, as the crumbing bodies surrounded me, crowding out my view of the night sky.

I hacked and clawed until the foul taste of ghoul was bound to be burned into my tongue for days. Eventually, they stopped coming. The ground below me had sunken considerably. I heaved a breath, lying down for a moment of rest and looking up at the dual moons and brilliant stars of home. I gave thought to staying longer, but I knew better. Faery was unpredictable on the best of days, and relentless on her worst.

As I moved to extract myself from the depression in the earth, my foot slipped below the grass, landing against an unyielding surface. Reaching down and feeling around decaying body parts, my fingers gripped a wooden ... door? Tentatively I pulled, knowing full well something nasty, but hopefully edible, could be down there. Worn hinges loudly announced the reveal of the last resting place of Lev's body.

With a grunt I straightened up, my stomach rumbling.

A white envelope in his shirt pocket caught my eye, and I pocketed it before reaching down to haul him out.

Death had not made Lev lighter, but heavier. I dragged his bloated ass back toward the car.

All the while I was waiting, straining my hearing for whatever had created all those ghouls, or whatever would be coming to see what all commotion was. Certainly, in this corner of Faery, something would come knocking.

I just wanted to eat it.

The amethyst sky shifted, a gentle and slow progression into turquoise light, glittering gold pieces dancing before my gaze. The darkened trunks of the ever-moving trees stilled, and the ground itself expelled thickening blood.

I was impressed. Dropping Lev's foot to clap loudly, I strode into the scene of horror. Slowly, he appeared, deadly sharpened teeth first, then thick brows, and eyes that perfectly mirrored in the sky.

"Next time, you should stain those pretty boys," I said, tapping my own teeth. "Gives it more authenticity."

A loud footfall had my stomach sinking. Please let that also be theater, I thought. I was tired.

The nostril that sniffed me deeply said it wasn't. I turned, raising an eyebrow at the winged giant, who grew in size before me. Irritation spiked through me, before a gleeful thought took its place.

"I can eat you!" I giggled, jumping up and down.

The blackened beast with rivers of red running over his body tilted his head at me and I lunged, pressing my hands into the cracks of his black armor and sucking. He growled, shoving me away and bending my body uncomfortably against a tree, which promptly spat out its old bones, hoping to add mine to the collection.

"Not today, asshole," I hissed, twisting out from the thorns poised as teeth.

The winged beast dropped down to all fours, smoke pouring from its nostrils before it spewed fire at me.

"Dammit!" I jumped to the side, covering my head, knowing that hair never grew back correctly after being fried off. Rolling, I was up and running at the beast before it could draw a second fire-spewing breath. With a lunge and a bellow of rage, I slammed my first down, breaking through its defenses and sucking for all I was worth.

That would be an epic joke to make later, but for the moment, the red veins burned my skin, sizzling my flesh. The horrid odor and rising, blackened smoke warred with my concentration to continue withdrawing its life force. The being shuttered once, trying to dislodge me, before turning into a husk of its former glory. My eyes felt electrified, my skin hypersensitive, and yet still I drained it.

When all that remained was a paper-thin corpse, I flung it from my hand.

Striding over to the vehicle, I knocked on the door. "It's me, and I have a dead body," I announced, oh so gracefully.

...

Bray and Seth took turns looking back at me in the car. "Are you sure you feel okay, Andy?" Bray asked for the tenth time.

"Fine," I replied, annoyed.

"You're glowing," Seth added.

"I'm aware. It's the power I pulled. My body will digest it," I shrugged. "At least it healed the bite marks," I commented idly.

"Bite marks?" Bray squeaked out.

"Yes, ghouls. Whoever is hunting you sure has an affinity for them," I commented, seeing a gas station coming up. "Can we get more pig skins?"

...

Tomolin looked at me, then back to Lev's head, now reunited with his body. I crunched on a pig skin.

"People don't typically eat in here," he muttered.

I shrugged, taking another loud bite. "What does this autopsy do, exactly?"

"I cut open the body and look to see why it failed," Tomolin answered, rolling out an impressive set of cutting instruments.

"Those are pretty," I complimented him. He paused, looking me over again.

I took another loud bite of skin.

"Maybe we should wait upstairs. Andy, you need a shower," Bray pointed out.

I shrugged. "I need more clothing as well," I admitted.

...

Liz and Zander were waiting for us in our apartment. A sick sense of violation creeped up my spine.

"Are they allowed to be here?" I asked Bray, wondering how fast I could eat them, considering how full I was.

"No," Seth answered in a rumble. "Unless given previous permission or in an emergency situation, they don't have full access to an apartment."

"Leave, Seth. This is Fae business," Liz dismissed him, with a condescending wave.

Bray nodded to him, reaching up on her tiptoes to kiss his cheek. Whatever passed between them caused his folded arms to drop. He pinched her chin, dropping another kiss to her lips briefly.

"You're grounded," Liz announced, shaking her head at me. "It's too dangerous, at least until we know who you are."

"Excuse me?" Bray snapped.

Liz raised a brown eyebrow at her. "Did I stutter?"

"What is grounded?" I inquired.

"You're not to leave the apartment," Bray explained.

A snarl built in my chest. "You mean to imprison me?" I snapped.

Zander held up his hands in mock capitulation. "You shoved a dead eye down a Fae's throat."

"He was a useless excuse for a Fae. His kind in Faery would be eaten for sport," I hissed.

"And that's the problem." Liz rubbed her temples. "We don't know who you are, or how you have this knowledge. And until we do, you aren't to leave the U."

She nodded to Zander, who followed her toward the door.

"This will not end well," I growled. "No one forces me into imprisonment for making a Fae use a natural-born skill set."

Zander wheeled on me. "Define skill set. You made him eat an eye, a decaying eye!" he repeated, shivering his disgust, as though my supposed infraction was monumental.

"I didn't remove his genitalia, didn't skin him alive, nor did I even touch his tongue. Trust me, if I'd wanted to hurt the pathetic excuse for a necromancer, he wouldn't have been able to tattle on me after." The power I had consumed flooded my body, and I was tempted to see if I could rectify my mistaken mercy.

"This won't stand. I'll file with the Supernatural Council," Bray warned softly.

"Do it, see how quickly they get back to you," Liz chuckled. "Fae are our problem. You know that, Bray. No one wants to deal with us, except us."

Her gaze raked over my torn clothing and ripped shoes with an air of distain, a superiority I was tempted to take her head over.

Zander took another moment to shrug while Liz clipped out the door in her ridiculous stilts of shoes. "I know you are trying to help Bray, Andy—"

"And it worked," Bray added.

Zander nodded, rubbing the back of his neck. "I know. Just give it time, she'll eventually calm down."

Bray and I shared a long look as he left.

"We're onto something," she hissed softly. "The fact they were both here means we are on the right path."

I sat down heavily on the couch. "Why would they want to prevent us from finding out who is trying to kill you?"

Bray shrugged. "I don't know, but if we were just spinning our wheels, you can bet no one would have given a shit. The fact that the heads of the Fae were here has to mean something."

"I'm not staying in this apartment," I warned her, fully prepared for her to revolt at my inability to follow their rules. "Simply because they are afraid of me and what I might be, that isn't a reason I'll stand to be imprisoned. Actually, I'm not sure I'd accept any reason."

She smiled, "I never dreamed of it."

...

"I dislike this more than the prison," I hissed from under a heaping pile of dirty laundry from the U's cleaning service. Bray did a poor job of containing her laugh.

"I really can't blame you," she hissed out in hysterical laughter. "Almost to the truck."

She rolled me into the back of a laundry truck and I heard Seth rumble, "You owe me."

"Payment later tonight," she teased.

"Yes," he rumbled to her laughter, closing the rolling door of the delivery vehicle as Bray hopped into the driver's seat.

We pulled away from the U and I was glad for her ingenuity and Seth's access to a variety of vehicles. Although I would admit neither.

"You're good!" Bray called out after a few turns.

"Thank all the Gods," I muttered, extracting myself from the foul smelling laundry.

Seating myself next to her, I sniffed my shirt. "That's horrid," I grunted.

Bray laughed, "I know, all the more reason this shopping trip is exceptionally needed."

"Where does Seth live?" I asked, looking out the window.

"At the shifter, uh, ranch," she smiled, clearly thinking about him. "He gets made when I called it a compound."

"What is the difference?" I asked, checking my jeans for additional stains.

"Compound implies that those who live there can't leave, or only can with permission from the alpha, which isn't true. But calling it that pisses him off, which makes me laugh. Ranch is more accurate, as it's really just a place where shifters are safe together, protected, and accepted," she finished wistfully.

"Aside from the current threat of murder, why don't you live there?" I asked, satisfied in my inspection.

Bray huffed, "It's complicated." She expertly maneuvered the large van around a corner. "That's a big, giant, moving-in-together step. Like he'd know where I am, 24/7—all the time," she corrected, guessing that I'd ask for clarification. "It's not that I don't trust him, I do, but he's male and a shifter. I don't pretend he's looking for forever with a half-fae."

"Have you asked him?" I questioned.

"No, I like how we are right now. I'm not looking to change it."

I nodded. "Could you breed?"

Bray hit the brakes in the parking lot, hard enough to jerk me from my seat. "Excuse me?"

"Ouch," I complained. "Could you a, half-fae, and him, a lycan, produce children?"

She continued to stare at me, mouth agape.

"Certainly, you must have thought of it before," I chided her.

"We use protection," she snipped, opening the van door.

I met her at the back of the van with a raised eyebrow. "Then you have thought about it."

"Half-fae are not fertile," she replied.

"Lycans?" I persisted.

"Are," she grunted.

"I hope you have furry babies," I gave her a giant smile.

"We are very close to not being friends right now," she hissed at me.

...

The mall was giant maze of winding aisles and clothing that all looked remarkably similar after not too long. Bray would only let me buy from the racks labeled CLEARANCE, explaining that it wasn't worth investing full price in an outfit I was going to ruin with bodily fluids or blood tears.

It was hard to argue with that logic.

We stopped for lunch in the food court, with a variety of greasy options.

"Pizza," she proclaimed, delivering the triangular slices with a flourish.

I tested the cheese with a finger. "I think I'd prefer the beast from last night."

The couple next to us looked over with widened eyes. I gave them my best toothy smile, before they quickly looked away.

"Trust me," she intoned, "pizza, one of Earth's seven greatest wonders."

I hesitantly took a bite, the greasy cheese dripping down my chin. "Mmmm, tell me of these other six wonders."

The pizza was followed by sugar-filled donuts, which were followed by a visit to a chocolate shop, which was immediately followed by sour stomachs.

"No more wonders," I grunted, holding my pained middle.

Bray dropped her packages into the back of the truck with a grunt. "Agreed. I'm now hoping to throw up."

"That would be a considerable improvement over our current situation," I agreed as I lounged in the passenger seat, waiting for her to slide in on the driver's side.

"You could at least turn it on," Bray scolded, growing weary of my love of being driven around. I caught the keys that she tossed up between the seats, leaning over to crank the engine, having watched her do that enough to mimic. I adjusted the AC, which in my mind was the most impressive invention humans had created.

"What the—ANDY!" her high-pitched scream of raw terror cut through me, ripping me to my feet. I rounded the space between the seats with a bellow of rage, lunging for the white metal doors that were being rolled violently shut in my face.

With a snarl, I slammed my body into the metal, hearing it creak under my forceful weight. A blast of magic from my hands that I didn't understand, nor give any thought to analyzing, burst the door from its track.

I tracked the scent of rubber to the black vehicle racing out of the parking lot. I wasn't faster than a speeding vehicle. That I knew for certain about myself.

But I had the keys. I had the keys!

Let her go, whispered the voice, with a seductive allure. *Who cares if one half-breed dies? We've killed plenty,* it chuckled.

I slid into the driver's seat, slamming my foot against the gas pedal, but nothing happened. The gear shifter, right, the shifter. Forcing the stick into drive against protesting metal, I hit the gas again and the van jerked forward, crashing into the car in front of me. Trying the "R" I had better success, narrowly avoiding a second collision with a car behind me.

My gaze anxiously searched for the black vehicle among the sea of drivers and bellowing horns.

There!

It was about to gain entrance to the highway that Bray loved so. Cutting around the line of cars to make a right turn, I was greeted by more horns and the squealing of brakes as I skidded around the corner, pressing the pedal to the floor, swerving around the cars and terrified drivers in my way.

The kidnappers spotted me, not that was I attempting to be discreet, and increased their own speed. Clipping the slow-moving vehicle in front of me, I swerved around, ignoring the lines on the ground in my desperate attempt to get Bray back.

The black vehicle exited the highway, cutting across four lanes of traffic. I followed a second later, to the sound of more horns and screeching tires.

I saw Bray in the backseat, eye blackened and swollen shut, kicking and fighting against the two men in masks who held her down.

Where was Seth when I needed him?

"Hey phone, call Seth," I yelled to my purse. Silence greeted me. I groaned, of course that would have been far too simple.

We barreled around another corner, and while the angry red eye of the light glowed above us, the black car careened through. It took a hit to the driver's side, screeching metal rewarding the driver's unfortunate decision. Slamming on the other pedal to stop, I rapidly changed my mind when the driver's door flung open. I had anticipated a hit with such force would incapacitate him. I was wrong, as the door flung open and he stood in his full and impressive height.

I increased my speed, pinning the rather large asshole between the van's bumper and the car door.

I let myself enjoy his last rasped breath with a smile, before ripping my own door open and scrambling around to the undamaged side of the kidnappers' car. A gasp stopped my movement, as a piercing pain radiated through my left shoulder. I blinked, dumbfounded.

Another popping sensation, and my stomach was ruptured in pain. Placing a shaking hand over the wound, I looked down in confusion at the bruised purple blood flooding out. My motions dragged, my mind slowed, my body was weakening.

Fool, chided the voice.

"Andy!" Bray screamed from the backseat, slamming her palm into the nose of one attacker, while the other turned the gun to Bray's temple. Gun. It would end Bray, of that I had no doubt. She stilled, obviously having thought the same.

A bystander approached. "Ma'am do you need help?" His voice carried concern.

"Call Seth, and cover your ears," I whispered softly on an exhale, before I sucked in a breath and screamed. The cry of the banshee, the wail of the dead and still walking.

The gunman dropped his weapon, clenching his hands over his ears as they bled. The car door crunched and broke away under my rallying show of strength. I constricted my hand around the gunman's neck, digging my fingers into the soft flesh, and sucked the life from him.

But it wasn't enough.

Staggering back, I looked down at my stomach wound. "Run, Bray. I can't protect you," I whispered, my back connecting with a solid surface of the van, my body sliding down to rest against the asphalt.

"NO!" Bray screamed, scrambling from the car to kneel in front of me.

"No," she repeated, tears welling in her eyes. "Andy, stay with me, please," she whispered, cradling my face.

Coldness was seeping into my body, taking with it my vision. My tongue thick in my mouth, I couldn't even repeat the warning to her.

What a waste, the voice whispered.

I had to agree.

…

My steps echoed through the castle, nary a maid nor serving boy in sight.

Kolm came from a corridor to my right, strapping on his sword. "Feeding?" I questioned with a raised caramel eyebrow.

"Always, weren't you?" he asked, wiping the lipstick smudge on his cheek.

"I had to check on something for Father," I answered, the strain in my voice evident.

"Something is going on with him," Kolm grunted.

"Quiet," I warned softly, "the walls have ears."

He raked a hand through his blond hair, streaked with honey highlights that matched my own. "I'm just tired of fighting. We've taken over the Spring Court and sent that bastard to an eternity in the ground." He laughed at that memory. "Bulked up our food supplies, not to mention the coffers, and killed off the lesser castes weakening Faery."

"Kolm," I warned softly, as we approached the war room.

He nodded, shoulders back, facial expression restrained and distant.

160

I nodded, pushing open the heavy oak doors.

"You've called for us, Father?"

"Daughter," our Father greeted us. I nodded to him, noting the way his gaze took in the cherry dress I had donned, and the matching lipstick.

"I hope I didn't interrupt your feeding." His hair matched our own perfectly, and the smile that curled his lips held no remorse or inclination of feeling. But lately his looks, and his hints, had bordered on incest. A prospect that curled my stomach, and confirmed my bother's suspicions that something was indeed off with him.

"Not at all," my brother seamlessly supplied. "What are we looking at?" Kolm asked, as we both took in the map before us.

"Autumn Court," my Father announced. He was watching us, with sharp blue eyes and a hawk nose. Any weakness he'd destroy in us, as he had in the past.

I nodded. "You plan to attack from the North?" I offered, giving Kolm a chance to calm his nerves before responding.

I watched our Father, eyes deadly locked on his only living son, examining the war board laid out on the table.

Kolm finally nodded. "It's a narrow pass, but if we can move through it quickly, we will have the benefit of surprise." He pointed to the closest town, and I could already taste the copper, smell the fires. "It'll take days for the news to reach the Autumn King to build a proper response." Kolm looked at Father. "They will never expect us, so soon after taking Spring."

Father smiled, showing genuine pride in his offspring. "Let us celebrate! Tomorrow we march!" he cried out. Out of necessity and part habit, Kolm and I joined our voices. Thankfully, Father wasn't paying enough attention to see that our hearts weren't in it.

After a copious amount of drinking and retelling beloved war stories, Father went to the concubines to feed his never-ending appetite.

From my quarters, I looked out over the Summer Court. The feast had been set outside the castle, and everyone was rejoicing at the King's lust for land and power. It unsettled me, in every space.

"My lady," a voice called out from the bedroom. "Do you plan on joining the peasants down there, or can I make you scream now?"

I looked back at the naked man with quite an impressive erection, stroking himself leisurely in my bed. Dropping my red dress to the floor, I stepped to him. "Let's see what you can do."

Chapter 15

I woke with a start, jerking against the handcuffs securing me to the metal railing. My stomach clenched as I sat up, and I cried out, my bleary eyes taking in the white room and the white gown I was dressed in.

With a jerk I snapped the metal cuffs, standing unsteadily. It took a moment for my gaze to translate what I was seeing. Behind thick glass, Liz stood, arms crossed over an ivory dress with fine detail pearl work. My gaze moved up to her gold crown, matching in its design. Stumbling, I made my way for the door between us, jerking hard on it but finding it locked, substantially so.

She watched me, the brown eyes crinkling in mirth, while I slammed, banged, and attempted to throttle the unbreakable door. Bent over, holding my stomach, I shuffled over to the glass.

"What have you done?" I bellowed in rage, and exceptional amounts of pain.

She clicked a button on the wall before speaking. "You really should have listened," she began with a smile. "You are now, truly, my prisoner."

"You won't get away with this," I hissed, slamming my fists against the glass, testing its resistance.

She flinched, a snarl replacing her smile. "Who's going to stop me?" She looked around at the indeed deserted torture lab she had spawned. "Bray?" she laughed. "She wasn't even at the scene when we arrived." Her gaze raked over the blood pooling from my wound. "Just you, bleeding out, having feasted on two humans, and the cause of numerous car accidents." She shook her head in disgust. "Now I'll have to use the fun drugs, so the healer can tend to your wounds."

"I won't take them," I growled at her, staggering to the hospital bed, my strength abandoning me yet again.

Another button was depressed and Liz shrugged. "Good news, you don't have a choice," she announced in a singsong voice.

The smell of the air changed and I coughed, feeling the effects immediately. She waved one hand at me before striding away. I fought for consciousness, for my freedom. But Liz was right; whatever she had let into the air, I was no match for it.

...

Days and nights passed in the fluorescent-illuminated hell. While food was delivered three times a day, Liz either didn't know or didn't care that I needed soul energy as well to survive. At this point, I was guessing she as well aware, and choosing to starve me slowly.

It's what I would have done. The voice was coming more frequently now. And with no one else to speak to, I found myself answering.

"Why?"

A message to enemies: obey or die.

"I don't think Bray and Seth would agree with that logic," I muttered, resting my back against the white wall.

They are expendable, and should be since neither listens well.

"They're our friends," I reminded the voice.

We don't need friends, the voice hissed. *What we need is our freedom.*

...

The dreams were getting worse.

My sandals made no noise on the black stairs as I followed Father down into the bowels of the castle.

Kolm had disappointed him, and was left to tend to his wounds from Father's lesson.

164

"Quiet, woman," Father chided the concubine, this one heavy with his child, leading us ever down into the pit where Magnus rested.

My stomach churned and my jaw felt wired shut. This didn't bode well. I just wasn't sure which of us I felt worse for. Father flicked his fingers and torches illuminated the dark, a handy skill he had inherited from the Spring Court, since its true King was now locked underground in a stone cell.

All too soon, we arrived at the throne Father had constructed down there so he could watch over Magnus, the oldest and most magical of all the dragons. The pit below the throne was swallowed in darkness. Father took his place on the bronze monstrosity, turning to look down at the concubine and me.

"Cut the babe from her and feed it to Magnus. I need information." He turned away from us.

"Father, you're talking about my half-sibling," I reminded him.

He sneered, revealing rows of sharp teeth, as his blue eyes glowed fiercely. "The bitch slept with half the warriors. The child isn't mine. I'd feel it."

"You gave me to them! You told me I had to!" the concubine screamed, her fists slamming against her thick thighs. "You can't do this! I come from an important family in the Shadow Land! You promised them I'd be safe here, that no harm would come to me!!"

My Father looked down at her with a shrug. "Who would defy me now?" He spread his arms wide. "Who would dare to try and kill me?"

Her eyes widened, and she stepped back. I fought down the urge to help her as she inched closer to the edge and Magnus.

Father snapped his fingers again, and the giant head of Magnus rose from the depths. Onyx eyes glittered, reflecting the torchlight behind us. His scales were an alluring swirl of azure, teal, and forest green. He tiled his head to Father, before snorting smoke over us from his long snout.

The concubine coughed, covering her mouth from the sulfur smell. I ground my jaws together, painfully, the rancid air trapped in my lungs.

"Begin, daughter."

I moved my body automatically to conjure my small blade, typically held in my boot. With a bronze handle and blue jewel on the end, it had been a present from Father on my thirteenth birthday, along with matching dual swords.

Her brown eyes rounded as she tried to ease away, her back foot sending rocks sliding over the pit's edge. Realizing now she was trapped, realizing she had no way out. That orders would be followed and her baby would be slaughtered.

I had killed thousands for my Father—including children—ending entire clans for his amusement. I had never once thought of killing him, but in this moment I wondered, could I do it? Was I strong enough?

The heavy burden of what he had tasked me with crushed my chest, decimating my heart. I slipped into the dark space of my psyche that I always retreated to, because while I was a murderer, I was also a survivor.

...

I awoke to the feeling of blood on my hands and crying in my ears. My head pounding, sweat dripping down my back, I pressed up against the hospital wall.

"Don't hurt me," whispered a small voice.

It took me many times blinking to finally clear my vision enough to see who spoke. A child with thick chestnut hair looked at me, dirt smeared under her eyes.

"Don't I know you?" I wondered, hunger clouding my brain.

She nodded. "You rescued me."

"Why are you here?" I asked, my confusion plain.

"That bitch said you are going to eat me. Please don't eat me!" she wailed, a fresh wave of tears flowing down her cheeks.

I shook my head. "I'll die first. You have nothing to worry about."

She sniffed, wiping her nose on the back of her sweater sleeve.

"You were supposed to go home," I said. At least, that was the version of the story I had created in my mind.

She shrugged. "They couldn't find my parents, and no one at the foster homes had room."

"Where have you been?" I asked.

She shrugged, picking at her sweater.

"You must have been somewhere?" I demanded, needing the distraction from my own woes.

"At this pompous bitch's house. She said she was trying to make me into a lady, whatever that means." Her brow furrowed, but I had the idea she knew something of it.

"We have to get you out of here," I grunted, standing up to pound on the glass.

Liz showed up instantly. I didn't need the girl to clarify who the bitch was. We agreed on that description.

"Get her out of here, she doesn't deserve this jail cell," I hissed at the glass.

Liz tsked at me. "Oh, Andy." She hit my name hard, and I narrowed my eyes in response. "It'll be so sad when you eat little Jazzy over there." Wiping away imaginary tears, she bitched on, "Which would be the reason I had to chain you up, since you are a child killer in your half-starved state." Liz's smile was pure predator. "No one will want you then, and things can progress as I need them to."

"What are you talking about?" I hissed.

I could hear Liz's foot tapping away. "You, Andy. You," she growled. "You in the human world needed to happen. Your..." She looked me over in disgust as she chose the words, "...your blatant disregard for life, your penchant for destruction. You are death walking, and I need you here to make it all happen."

"You're talking in circles," I ground out, a wave of dizziness flowing over me, my stomach cramping painfully.

"Maybe I should give you back your memories. Maybe that was my mistake." Her eyes narrowed on me, foot tapping annoyingly.

"YOU took my memories?" I hissed at her. "Why?" I laughed, barbing her. "And you did a shitty job, because I keep dreaming them." I smirked at her irritated scowl.

"Okay then, maybe that's actually the solution here, to wipe your memories again," she mused thoughtfully. "I should just send you back. You are nothing but a FRUSTRATING TIME WASTE," she ended on a scream, before pointing at the girl in the corner. "I'd suggest eating if you want to stay alive. I had this place built special, just for your kind of disgusting monster."

I shuffled back to my favorite corner, sliding down, listening to Liz's heels click off in the distance. "If you have any ideas, kid, I'm open."

She shook her head and I exhaled, looking at the ceiling and the grate screwed on there.

"It's too small," she whispered.

I nodded, but there had to be something. Some angle I had missed, some fact about myself that could get us out of there. Too bad I couldn't summon the banshee wail again. I hardly had energy to walk around the small cell.

...

Screaming woke me, coming from outside the room where we were housed. The child had moved closer to me, watching through the glass as uniformed guards ran past. A snarling reached my ears and I pushed off the wall, staggering to stand and get a better look.

168

A large grey wolf with cobalt eyes gazed unblinkingly back at me. "Seth? Please be Seth," I groaned, wondering if I was now suffering from hallucinations.

He huffed one short bark and Bray came up behind him, along with an entire pack of large beasts.

Her smile was genuine, as were the tears shinning in her eyes. "We're getting you out of here."

"There's a girl in here with me. She needs help, too." I leaned heavily against the glass.

"Andy?" Bray screamed, slamming her hand against the glass. "Stay with me!" she demanded through wide, worried eyes.

"Kid? Kid? You have to help her!" Bray screamed, pounding the thick glass between us.

The girl came to my side. "She's starving, what to do want me to do? Be her fucking happy meal?"

I sighed. "She's not wrong. See if you can keep a few guards alive for me," I wheezed out in an attempt at a joke.

Seth barked a few times, and I honestly wondered if he would do what I had requested.

It felt like an eternity that I held myself up against the glass, watching Bray try and fail again and again to open the door. We were so close to freedom, so close. A fresh wave of gunfire erupted, and the door swung open as she ducked.

Without thought, I dragged the girl through the threshold before shoving her to Bray, my movements so efficient, so deadly. I didn't remember making them, and still don't. One moment I was locked in a cell with no hope of escaping, the next, two guards hung as husks of their former selves in my hands. It wasn't enough, though, and I pushed for more, taking down another four as easily as blinking.

"Andy!" Bray screamed at me.

I turned back to look at her. "We have to go!" she yelled.

"I'm going to kill them all." My voice sounded so far away, as though I wasn't quite in control. I didn't feel in control, either. Something else had come out to play, and she was doing an exceptional job.

Six more guards and I found myself full, but compartmentalizing the energy.

Had you done this previously, that bitch couldn't have contained us.

Oh good, the crazy person in my brain was taking over. Excellent. More gunfire and I rounded the corner, consuming the man with brilliant green eyes, watching as they faded in death. Exquisite.

"No! Andy, we have to go, NOW!" screamed Bray again, panicked.

I turned, seeing Seth limping behind her, blood dripping from his side.

My back, they had been protecting my back.

LEAVE THEM she hissed.

"Shut up, bitch," I muttered, coming to Seth's side. I laid my hands on him, funneling the energy, the healing into him, pushing out the bullets and reknitting the muscles and flesh.

When I looked into his cobalt eyes, he blinked once. "Don't get hurt again, unless you have a feast for me," I warned, eerily emotionless.

He blinked, slowly backing up.

"Follow me! Well," I amended, "direct me, but stay behind. I'll ward the rear."

...

We were in another large, white van, huddled in the back with several naked men. The girl's face flushed and I cursed.

"Child, no one will hurt you here," I reassured. She still didn't look at me, arms wrapped tightly around her legs, but everyone made space and I moved to sit next to her amidst the sausage fest currently happening.

"How did you heal Seth?" a blond-haired man asked. His power washed over me, and I noted he was handing out sweats as he also covered himself up.

"It's a power balance. Our bodies require energy to heal. The more energy applied, the faster the healing happens." I shrugged. That seemed the simplest explanation. "Who are you?"

"I'm Rohn, the pack alpha. So, you sucked the energy out of the guards?" he questioned, blue eyes watching me.

"I did."

"And pushed it into Seth," he clarified.

"Correct."

"Hmmm."

...

We drove for hours as I watched the city fall away, and the countryside replace it.

"How did you find me?" I asked of Rohn.

"The kid you told to call Seth?" he began.

I tilted my head, thinking back on that event. It felt so long ago, but I nodded for him to continue.

"He's pack, so he knew who Seth is and called him." He shifted uncomfortably in the cramped space. "Bray wouldn't leave you, and Liz was en route. The kid had to throw her over his shoulder to get her to safety. There wasn't time to come back for you."

I didn't blink, holding my gaze fixed on him.

She left you behind to die, the voice raged at me.

"She came back," I informed her.

"Yeah, she did," Rohn agreed, not realizing that I was a crazy person talking to a voice. "We all did. We're the Northern Territories Pack, and we just put a huge target on our backs by coming for you." He shrugged, "Bray said you are worth it."

I blinked. "I'm not."

He was taken aback by that comment, but before he could respond, the vans parked and back doors were ripped open. I squinted at the daylight streaming in.

"Andy!"

People shifted positions, shooing me out of the van. "Oh, Andy!" Bray's arms came around to lock in me in an awkwardly returned hug. "I'm so sorry I left you. I never should have." Tears slipped down her face.

"I told you to run," I reminded her. "No good would have come from us both being captured."

She pulled back, hands going into her jacket pockets as she tearfully nodded. I placed a hand on her bicep. "Thank you for coming for me," I whispered.

"Anytime," she nodded. Clearing her throat, she turned to look at the girl. "I thought we already rescued you," she questioned, confused.

"Liz kept her, apparently trying to teach her how to be a lady?" I offered with a shrug.

Bray's gaze narrowed. "That doesn't make any sense."

I sighed, dropping even more information that didn't make any sense. "Liz took my memories. She wants me to do something, cause something." I shrugged, "I have no idea what."

"That is great news! If she took your memories, she can give them back."

I sighed heavily, following the others to the massive house in the center of the compound—ranch, I corrected myself."I don't think I want them," I admitted.

Everyone around me turned to stare, and I shook my head."I don't think I was a good person in Faery," I admitted.

"Why?" Bray asked. "Because you're hearing voices? That could be a side effect of the curse, or your hunger."

"Because of the memories I dream of," I answered softly.

"There's no way to tell if they are yours," Bray argued.

"They are mine. I know those moments intimately. I know part of what I've done," I acknowledged with a slow shake of my head, "and I don't wish to recall more."

Bray was silent. The entire clan poured into the home and instantly, food was being passed around.

"Where is Seth?" I asked.

"He's at the doctor, getting checked out." She held her hands up to stop my protest. "Not that we doubt your supreme ability to heal, but just to be sure."

I nodded. "Was anyone else hurt?"

"Not to that extent," Bray answered.

"How did you get the entire clan to show up? Did you lie to them?" I questioned.

Bray smiled. "I told them the truth, that a Royal High Fae had saved my life and been abducted." She grimaced with a gleam in her eye. "And I maybe bribed Seth."

I chuckled. "I don't know how I can repay these people," I said softly, as a few heads turned to us. "I have nothing of value to offer."

Bray cleared her throat. "Yeah, about that. I think they have an idea."

"Which is?"

"Bray," a voice broke in. I turned, seeing Rohn. "Let me explain it."

Chapter 16

I looked across at Rohn, seated behind his massive oak desk, hands steepled in front of him, intelligent eyes regarding me solemnly. He had warded the room against eavesdropping with crystals, which made sense amidst a population with exceptional hearing. Bray sat next to me, watching my reactions closely.

"Summing up, you want me to kill Liz?" I clarified.

"Correct," Rohn stated, waiting for my reply.

"Why?" Truthfully, I was planning on ending the bitch, anyway.

Rohn sighed, running his hands through his blond hair before meeting my gaze. "We've had our suspicions for a while. The U isn't the only place that likes to hire shifters for security, and while the assumption might be that we're big, beefy, and dumb, my people pay attention. They've noticed Fae leaving the building with humans, and then both disappearing. We are the ones who alerted them to Cameron."

His shoulders sank as he raked though his hair again. "And while quite a few humans were rescued, it wasn't all, not even half. While you were playing with Liz, we were able to fill in the missing pieces, namely that Liz is running an underground Fae slavery ring. Both the humans and the lesser Fae are being forced into slavery."

"Slavery?" The word was slippery over my tongue.

"No control over their bodies or what they do. It's bad, Andy," Bray expanded.

I nodded.

"Why have you been waiting for me to do it?" I questioned. Certainly, a lingering problem of this magnitude would warrant a swift response.

Rohn kicked his legs up, resting his feet on his desk.

"Our normal avenues of recourse aren't available to help. The Supernatural Council and national shifter leadership see this as a Fae problem, requiring a Fae solution. If we were to intervene, we ourselves would be held liable," Rohn answered.

So I was a Fae solution for a Fae problem.

"Why do you think I can kill Liz?" I questioned his logic. "She apparently stole me from Fae and took my memories." I was actually confident I could kill the bitch, and I'd enjoy killing her. I might even draw on some of the memories beginning to haunt me.

"You are a powerful Fae," he answered.

"Everyone says that like it means something of value," I grumbled.

Bray scoffed a laugh. "Yeah, it means you can track killers by licking the dead, set impressive wards, and eat soul energy."

"And those things are … unusual," I ended on a sigh.

She nodded, "Highly."

"But she still had the upper hand on me at one point," I reminded them both. I did wonder how that happened, and what my memories might be just before she snatched me to this planet.

Rohn dropped his feet with a thud, leaning forward and causing his chair to groan. "She won't this time. My people have been watching her and in three weeks, she will be going to her favorite spa, one where she leaves her guards at the doors and shuts down, just for herself. That's where you'll kill her."

"How do we get in?" Bray asked.

I shot her a glance. What was with this *we* stuff?

"We have a masseuse on the inside, she'll let you in."

"And after Liz is dead?" I asked.

"What do you mean?" Rohn questioned, spreading his hands out wide. "We slay the dragon and win."

"What is life like in your simple world?" I asked him, my head cocked to the side. "Who takes over for Liz governing the Fae? And will that person continue to traffic innocent victims? Do you have full proof of an alibi for yourself? You did just save me, people will be suspicious. What's my story if caught?"

Rohn's scowl deepened.

"We need to strike at the trafficking first, then kill her and figure out who you want to replace her," I educated him. I found myself wondering how many times I had offered such enlightenment previously.

"Zander?" Bray offered.

Rohn scoffed, before shrugging, "He's the next in line, but he'll be after whoever killed his sister."

Bray nodded at the truth in that statement. "Besides, he may be in on the whole thing," Rohn added.

I nodded, "Quite possible."

Silence crept over us for a few moments, before my newfound wisdom forced its way out of my mouth again. "If you create a power vacuum, you must be ready to fill it," I instructed Rohn.

"Fine," he snapped. "I'll take care of it."

"Are you prepared to end Zander as well if he scents our trail?" I demanded.

Rohn nodded, "I am."

"Excellent, let's go hunt down a trafficking."

"Trafficking *ring*," Bray corrected.

"Whatever, let's go kill stuff." I desperately needed the distraction from memories running rampant.

"This is Liz's house?" I whispered to Bray, while we slipped through the lush grounds of the extravagant mansion.

Gently, I nudged her, pointing to a red flower. "That's a garden Fairy," I pointed out. With wonder in her gaze, she bent town to take in the slender Fairy staring up at her.

"She's so dainty," Bray murmured, waving hello.

The dainty little Fairy took a deep breath, her red-lipped mouth opening wide before I slammed my hand down, knocking her out.

"What the hell, Andy?" Bray hissed.

"It's also an early warning system," I amended.

"That would have been helpful to know," she hissed.

I shrugged, "This was far more entertaining." With a signature eye roll, she turned away from me.

The question was, and still is, how Liz was moving the Fae around. The facility Bray and friends had saved me from was no longer operational, which made sense if Liz was still trying to keep up the façade of being ruler of the Fae. Meanwhile, I was still being painted as the deranged, unknown Fae who tried to kill everything, which might have been accurate.

"Its remarkably boring here," I grunted to her.

Bray huffed. "It's been maybe six minutes. The intel from Rohn said it would be thirty minutes before we can get inside to where Jazzy was being kept. It's our best lead on where Liz is holding people." She scoffed, "It's both smart and sick that she's scooping up kids in the foster system who don't have families."

"Right. Remarkably boring," I repeated. It was true, nothing happened. A few guards patrolled the grounds, but with the invisibility ward I had in place, they didn't notice us laying in wait.

"Stop knocking out the Fairy!" Bray scolded.

"She's going to tattle on us. I could kill her instead," I added with a shrug.

"Fine, keeping knocking her out," she reluctantly agreed.

The braying of horses snapped my attention to the black night beyond the house. Hound calls followed.

"Bray," I hissed, ignoring the Fairy who now screamed an early warning, "RUN!" I pushed her hard through the underbrush, and away from what I knew was coming.

She stumbled before catching her footing, looking behind us.

"I told you to keep knocking it out!" she hissed at me.

"Don't you hear it?" I hissed back at her.

"The damn thing screaming? Yes, it's all I can hear!"

"No," I whispered, meeting her gaze before we sprinted across the street to her car, "the hounds are coming. The wild hunt has been released."

Bray's confusion made me want to shake her. "You've never heard of the wild hunt?" I hissed.

She shook her head, her movements far too languid for what approached. "The wild hunt is only the deadliest of Fae occupations. The hounds are infallible, always securing their target, no matter the causalities."

He calls the Wild Hunt. He's found us.

"And you think it's here from Faery?" Bray asked as we slammed car doors closed.

I nodded, "I know it is."

"How?" she asked, merging with traffic. "The Fae would have to move an entire hunting party through to our dimension."

I shook my head. "The Mistress of the Hunt follows the hounds, and she can rip portals into the air."

Bray looked over at me, shocked.

"She is powerful and beholden to the darkest of all the Fae," I added.

Bray slammed the car to a stop, throwing me a look before jamming the gear shift into reverse.

"We don't run from danger, Andy, we stop it. Innocents are going to be hurt."

"Bray," I whispered softly. "They're here for me. I cannot protect you from what is coming."

"Well, they can't have you, I just got you back!" She winked, "And I'm harder to kill than I look."

Every instinct in me warned me to run, to hide, and to never look back. And to take Bray with me. The darkness unfurling was going to destroy us all.

Run and hide! Father will kill us!

And that's exactly what finally made my decision for me. "Okay, let's go back." My hands clenched, searching for a weapon I was missing. "A sword would be handy," I muttered to myself.

First order of business, I was killing that bitch Liz, damn the consequences. At this point, I might not live long enough to see a successor, anyway.

Bray was on the phone. "Anyone you bring here is likely to die," I informed her, my emotions shutting down.

"Andy, they know, but they're still coming."

I nodded.

It won't be enough.

I refused to voice that dismal thought, even if it was right.

180

Chapter 17

My instincts screamed that this was the final stand. And if it was, I was taking out Liz first.

"You sure about this?" Bray hissed at me, her pistol drawn.

"I am," I answered, raising my booted foot to smash against the ornately carved wooden door, after dispatching its wards.

The husks of the guards wafted in the breeze, and my foot found purchase through the wood on my second attempt.

Bray reached through, flipped the lock, and opened the door, waving me in. I smiled at her. "Wait for backup," I warned her yet again. The glare she leveled at me adequately conveyed how poorly she thought of this strategy.

Perhaps she was right.

Blindly, I went through, laying the pack's elaborate plan to waste. But the debt I owned them sat unwell in my stomach. I didn't enjoy owing anything to anyone. Certainly, there was a memory lying in wait to plague me with reasons for that, pending I survived this encounter.

The familiarity of the home struck a cord, although I didn't have time to wonder why before the first attacks began. Liz utilized both Fae and human guards, who shot at me with their bullets. Learning from my mistake of thinking those were useless, I tossed up an energy shield.

The guards' surprise delighted me as the projectiles bounced harmlessly away. The first guard was close enough for me to shoot my left hand through his neck, draining until his body hung lifelessly in my grip, while my right forearm stayed up, shielding me.

Dropping the husk, I moved toward the Fae on the stairs, his white robe flowing around him as he created a wicked ball of power in his hands. He enlarged his hands to expand the ball once again, and then with a delighted and self-satisfied smirk on his pale face, released the energy.

It would be a waste, having the energy batter against my shield when it would have been so delightful to absorb. It grew into a ball of massive fire and I braced against it, the flames licking behind my shield to burn caresses against my cheek and down my neck.

The pain was familiar as it settled into me. Dropping my shield, I cleared the four steps to arrive next to his ear. "Pretty, but useless," I whispered, before extending my claws and capturing his heart. Energy flowed up my arm and into my body, throbbing in time to my own heartbeat as I consumed his life force.

A small voice whispered that I was adept at this, I was a born killer and that's all I could ever hope to be. I pushed it away; now was not the time to have a heart to heart with my need to kill to survive. The top of the imperial staircase flooded with additional humans, dressed alike in black suits, guns drawn.

I moved with the speed of thought, ripping out hearts and consuming souls. Nary a bullet was wasted.

I smiled, wiping the blood from my face before I began listening, a skill I had been woefully underusing in this realm. My hair floated around me, the life forces I'd consumed radiating as I neared my limit.

Three hearts to my left were beating wildly. I inhaled the scent of fear, kicking in the locked door to find three terrified Chitterans huddled in a corner.

My brow furrowed.

"What are you doing here?" I asked.

Not one looked at me. I stalked to them, dragging the male up by his pressed shirt. "I asked a question," I hissed.

He urinated himself.

"Disgusting." I tossed him back down, hauling up one of the females.

"What are you doing here?" I demanded again.

"We work here!" she screamed at me, eyes rolling back in pure terror. "We're forced to work here to pay for our families to come over. Please," she begged, grabbing ahold of my shirt, "please don't kill us, we didn't hurt the children." She sobbed, "We've tried to protect them!" Spittle flew from her furry face.

I dropped her whimpering form, making a snap decision. "Go outside and find Bray. Tell her where the children are, so she can save them."

Dumbfounded, she froze with her mouth hanging open. "I'd suggest hurrying. I can hear another wave of guards coming," I warned her. Not waiting for her to gather her wits, I left the room behind. I couldn't help but wonder why the hidden city of Chitterans had neglected to inform us that their own were being kept as slaves.

The next two rooms held nothing of interest, so I pushed back through the weighty center doors, kicking away the husks from my previous meal. A bullet grazed my shoulder and I tossed an energy ball at the offender, my hand still wishing for a sword I couldn't seem to manifest.

In the distance, the hounds called to each other, beginning to close in on me. I knew the fear that radiated up my spine was the Wild Hunt and not my own, but it still sent me against the nearest wall until I could get my breathing to even out.

The ghostly image of the Huntress wafted in my mind, her ice blond hair and piercing green gaze.

"Give me time," I sent on a whisper to the wind, "let me finish this." Whether she heard or not, I couldn't say, but enough moments passed that I was able to push off the cream-colored wall and fend off the next attack.

...

I was deep in the bowels of the mansion before I finally found something of interest, although it mortified my soul. The rooms down there were set up just like the warehouse Cameron had brought me to, where I had met Jazzy for the first time.

I ducked under the hanging chains, my miserable gaze fixated on the blood-stained bedsheets. The four-poster bed was exquisitely carved, with writhing forms in various positions of torture. I ran my fingers over the matching wooden hilts of various, carelessly forgotten torture devices.

I shouldn't have been surprised. It's too often those who vow to protect us, to keep us safe, who harm us. I doubted my lost memories held a single exception to that rule.

Fear hung in the air, thick and pungent. Catching the scent, I left the room, moving down the hallway.

The noises from the next room sounded depraved even by Fae standards, and I swung open the door, shattering the lock in the process.

Zander stood naked and sweaty, a bloody dagger secure in his hand. He didn't see me, his gaze solely focused on the woman on the bed and she, with her golden hair and piercing green eyes, felt strangely familiar.

"Get out!" the woman hissed at me.

I blinked. Competing visions overlapped, causing my temples to throb in time with my heart. Shaking my head to clear it provided no relief.

"Get out, Andy," the woman hissed again, although this time she solidified into Liz.

Zander, still erect, look mortified.

"What have you done?" He turned to me, anger vibrating from his sweat-covered body. Horror rounded his eyes as he demanded, "TURN HER BACK!"

"I didn't do anything," I countered, pointing at Liz, tied down spread eagle. "That is her true form." And, I recognized, a remarkably easy one to kill. Was I disappointed? I think I was.

185

"It was Andromalius!" Zander bellowed at me. "The bitch who took my powers. Turn her back NOW!"

"Andromalius," I whispered the name over my lips, feeling the physical blow from it.

"GET … OUT, ANDY!" Liz screamed, anger or lust making her pant between the words.

"No, I came here to kill you, and I'm not leaving until it's done."

"The hell you will." Zander advanced on me, the wicked dagger weaving toward my face. I ducked the blade, landing an uppercut against his well-defined abs.

"Did you really just fuck your sister?" I taunted him.

He roared sounds no ears could understand.

"You've ruined everything!" Liz screamed, fighting in earnest now against the white ropes binding her down.

"I'm going to kill you, Liz, and end the sick empire you have constructed on the backs of the people you were supposed to protect."

Zander lunged, attempting to expose my intestines to the fresh air. I backed up quickly. "Honestly, Zander, I don't mind taking you out as well."

Two quick hits to his kidneys, and he went down on a knee. A snap of my leg forced his other knee to the floor. Without looking, I pulled a black-handled blade from his expansive collection, placing it against his throat.

"Andy, stop!" Liz's high-pitched cry pierced my eardrums.

I turned us both, seeing all of her womanhood exposed.

"Give me a reason," I growled.

"I'll give you back your memories, and remove the curse," she pleaded, eyes glued to the glistening blade against her brother's neck.

"Nope, try again," I singsonged at her.

Her gaze met mine. "What do you want?" she finally screeched.

"The truth," I calmly demanded.

"Fine," she sighed, settling back against the pillow under her head. "In Faery, I tricked Zander into sleeping with me, under the guise of being you."

"Sick and twisted," I muttered.

She scoffed, "Don't pretend to be so high and mighty. The payment was that you got to watch me fuck my brother."

"I'm so glad to have refused the memories," I muttered.

"What?" Zander whispered.

"Don't pretend you didn't know," she reprimanded him. "You saw how my magic of the undead grew after that night. You knew."

"The hell I did!" Zander screamed. "Why? Why would you do this?" he demanded.

Liz shrugged, "To get what I want." She pulled at the ropes. "Had you just given in to what was between us, I could have given back your power, instead of having to enact this fucking circus to get you to touch me again!" she wailed at him.

I lined it all up in my head. Eliza had pulled me from Faery and taken my memories, all to get her brother to fuck her again. Ewwww. I felt dirty just knowing it. And I ate souls as a hobby.

Zander lunged and I sighed, holding him by his hair. "Enough, this ends."

I moved to slice the blade deeply into Zander's throat, but the wall exploded, jarring us all and tossing my body out the door, but not before I took half the entry with me.

Plaster rained down, the fine dust making its way into my lungs. I coughed, flat on my stomach, trying to remember how to move my legs.

Zander dashed for Liz, only to stop cold, as did my heart, the breath in my lungs refusing to move as I looked over the man from my nightmares.

Golden hair flowing around his shoulders, crimson battle armor accented with threads of gold adorning his body, his merciless blue eyes landed squarely on me.

We were so close, the voice whispered in sorrow, so close to truly being free. So close to leaving the horrors of Father behind us.

I could feel her hopes being ripped from our body, and agony replacing them. This man was nightmares made flesh.

"Daughter," his voice echoed, warm and dangerous.

I stood on shaky feet. "Who are you?" I asked softly, still in deep denial.

He blinked, shocked. "What have you done to my daughter, Eliza?" he growled.

"Nothing I can't fix!" she screeched, trying unsuccessfully to sink into the mattress and disappear.

He made his way to the foot of the bed, his gaze drawn by the blades Zander had forgotten about.

"Pretty," he remarked. Looking up, he locked his eyes onto Eliza or Liz. "Are you here to play, Eliza? With such exquisite tools, it's a wonder you never made it into my bed."

Eliza pulled on the white ropes, fear mangling her face, sobs refusing to break free.

"Please," she whispered, barely above a breath, "I'll fix her, I swear I can fix her."

"Who says I want her back?" my Father asked.

My brow furrowed.

"She's your daughter," Eliza whispered, watching Father expertly handle a short blade, dragging it up her calf to her inner thigh. He paused, leaning over Eliza's lips.

"I can make more," he grinned. The blade found a home and I cringed, her blind cry of pain piercing my ears.

Zander had started creeping backwards. Fool.

I stood my ground. I had no chance of killing my Father, but Liz-Eliza, her death was mine, and I announced as much.

Father turned crystal blue eyes to me. "You want her?" he asked.

"She's mine to kill," I told him again.

"Why?" he asked, going back to the tools of destruction at his disposal.

I knew that "Because I said so" wasn't going to win this argument, but I wasn't sure I had much else.

"Do you remember her?" he asked, pain clearly fracturing his mask of control.

"No, I only know that she did this to me, she took my memories."

"And killing her will grant you freedom?"

"I am free. Killing will grant me peace," I countered, trying for my best bravado.

He nodded, looking over the long and thin blade he had selected.

Slowly, he lowered his lips to her ear, as blood flowed freely from the wound he had inflicted. Liz whispered, pleading.

"Shhh," he whispered, placing a kiss on her lips. "Shhh, you must listen, pet."

Eliza shook her head, but he continued. "You are such a delightful package. I think I'll keep you and your brother alive." Zander's backward movement stopped, his body pulled by invisible strings. "I see you, Elias, trying to leave your sister to take the fall for your pathetic mistakes." Father tsked. "Weak,

weak, weak. You're lucky I want to see you fuck her ravenously." His gaze landed on Zander's now flaccid cock.

"Hmm, perhaps you need some motivation."

Father looked over to me as he pierced Eliza's nipple with the blade. "Now hush, you are going to return my daughter's memories. I need her by my side." He stroked Eliza's face delicately as he positioned the second nipple to take the same blade.

He growled with approval as she panted in pain.

I hate him. I hate the life he forced me into. I hate who I was, whispered the voice. Hopelessness and agony warred inside of me, along with a rage pure and beautiful.

Agreed, I answered.

"Please," Eliza rasped, "please."

"Yes, pet." Father toyed with the blade down below. "Tell me what you need."

I couldn't hear Eliza, but my rage boiled. I tried to move. I could kill her quickly and make this done. And hopefully, Father's rage would turn on me and he'd drag me back to Faery, or this world was doomed.

But I couldn't fucking move; pain flared in my shoulders as I tried.

He looked at me, his perfectly straight nose and shapely eyebrows rising in excitement, and with a single word. "Sleep," I dropped into fucking oblivion.

Chapter 18

"Awake."

It was my turn to be tied down, although at least someone had thought to use a different room, one not exploded by interdimensional travel.

Unlike Liz, I was held on a dial at an angle, and thankfully none of my clothing had been removed. An altar stood to my left, where Father stroked Liz-Eliza's hair gently, enjoying the tears that streaked her face as she sobbed out the incantation.

Fire laced my skull, arching my back off the wooden surface. No scream escaped me, the breath trapped in my lungs.

I sagged, dizzy and nauseous.

As Liz began chanting again, my jaws ground together. Every word she uttered was forced, pain brutally lacing her body and my own. Perhaps we both deserved it.

Drool dripped down my chin and tremors shook my body, my head dropping. And still the bitch kept fucking chanting.

The howl of hounds reached my ears, along with my Father's annoyed tsk. Apparently, he had gotten ahead of himself this Hunt. Although how he'd managed to find me remained a mystery.

Jarring pain seared through my temples, and I didn't recognize my own scream.

"Did you know, Elias, that the only reason I found my daughter was that your sister's greedy pussy demanded your cock?" Father moved toward Zander-Elias, still naked in a chair.

Father kicked his legs apart, leaving Elias helpless to cover or protect himself.

Bone-jarring pain erupted behind my eyes and I screamed until my throat was raw.

"Had Eliza not taken the form of my daughter, I never would have found her. Which brings me to the key question: Eliza, how did you alter my daughter's appearance?"

Panting, Eliza clung to the ancient text in front of her. "I removed her glamour … permanently," she added shakily.

Father nodded once. "So she'll be this mediocre creature forever?"

"She will," Liz hissed.

Father reached between her legs, and a cry escaped Liz. "Good girl," he crooned, "don't stop now."

The chanting reached a painful crescendo as Liz barreled ahead, my screams and hers drowning each other out. All the while, Zander looked on, dumbstruck. Wind from a forgotten realm stirred, and I could feel the pressure on my spine to submit and remember.

"NO!" I cried out, thrashing against the bonds. "NO!" I didn't want to be that person again. I didn't want to remain heartless my entire life. I wanted to feel, to love, to care.

"Why isn't it working?" my Father demanded in a growl.

Liz cried out, but my eyes could no longer see the torture he subjected her to. "She's fighting it," she sobbed out.

"Cut her down," Father demanded of Zander. "We will take this back to Faery."

The hounds picked that moment to descend upon us.

"Oh, the hell," Father huffed. "Fine, bring her along."

I cracked an eye open, seeing the one person I never wanted to know this hell.

Bray.

Cut down, I fell to my knees and summoned every ounce of strength in or around me. I might be going back to Faery and the shit of my nightmares, but Bray wasn't. Never. Her, I'd die to protect.

I launched myself at the guards, destroying them easily. The hounds were next, massive jaws with double rows of serrated teeth cutting into me. I kicked and punched through hearts, a spinning whirl of movement to protect her from them, and from *him*.

Bray couldn't save me from what was coming, no one could. But I could still save her.

Still more teeth bit into my flesh, dragging me through the portal and into the realm of my birth. Cool grass cushioned me there. I saw the white-haired Huntress gather her hounds, sorrow etched on her perfectly proportioned features, turning to anger as my Father sent her back to Shadow.

Each breath felt labored, as though weights were being added to my chest one by one. I heard before I saw the familiar clink of the armor of the Royal Guard.

"Bring her," Father commanded. Magic enveloped me, lifting my ravaged body to helplessly follow.

Epilogue

Bray sat on the futon in the empty apartment, the image of Andy being dragged through that portal haunting her.

With tears already coating her tongue, she pulled another drink from the bottle of whisky, using a tear-stained sleeve to wipe her mouth.

"Hey kid," Seth announced his arrival.

Bray grunted, acknowledging him.

"She's gone," Bray whispered.

Seth exhaled, taking the bottle from her before scooping her up into his arms. Bray was a fighter, but when he held her, he was reminded how small her frame really was.

"For now," Seth agreed.

"She just can't—" Bray's voice broke. "I just can't accept that she's Andromalius," she ended in a whisper.

Seth, nodded, tucking her head under his chin. "There were moments that make sense now."

Bray huffed, "Like when she made the necromancer eat the eye?"

"Exactly, and her knowledge."

They sat in silence together.

"I miss her," Bray confessed.

"I know, kid, you never let anyone in like that."

"I let you in," she reminded him.

Seth huffed a laugh. "I tend to think of it more as me beating the door down."

Bray gave him a small smile and shrug.

"She'll come back," Seth stated.

"How can you say that so confidently, when you saw the hounds drag her off?" Bray whispered. "And her father..." Bray shook, remembering the brief glimpse she had gotten of the madman.

"They didn't drag her." Seth took a deep sip of the whisky. "She let them take her."

Bray sat up straighter. "How could you say that? You saw her—the blood, the arm hanging off," she ended in a panicked whisper, closing her eyes against the gore-filled memory.

"She slowed her movements once she saw you," Seth answered, his gaze far away. "Just enough so it still took the entire pack to drag her back to Faery."

"So she picked us over her own freedom." Bray shook her head. "It's not right."

Seth sighed. "It's Faery, and neither of us can do a damn thing about it." Bray hung her head and Seth massaged the back of her neck. "But we can get down to the infirmary and help those kids we saved."

"In the morning," Bray whispered. "Tonight, I mourn."

Seth handed her back the bottle. "We mourn."

Connect with me!

Thank you so much for taking your precious time to read my novel! I truly hope you enjoyed reading it, as much as I enjoyed writing it!

Telegram: kimschubertauthor

Instagram: kimschubertauthor

Facebook: kimschubertwriter

Email: thekimschubert@gmail.com

www.ingramcontent.com/pod-product-compliance
Lightning Source LLC
Chambersburg PA
CBHW022104170626
46808CB00002B/596